Animal Attraction

A paranormal erotic romance novella collection by
Michelle Houston

ANIMAL ATTRACTION

www.unleashedink.com

ANIMAL ATTRACTION

Cover art © 2014 Michelle Lee
www.michelleleedesigns.net

Edited by Jenna Byrnes and D. Musgrave

Published by Unleashed Ink

This is a work of fiction. Names, places, characters and incidents are either the product of the author's imagination or are used fictitiously, and any resemblance to any actual persons, living or dead, organizations, events or locales is entirely coincidental.

This book is dedicated to the dreamers …

* * *

It goes without saying that in any writing endeavor, there are those that are behind the scenes that make writing possible. To all who have assisted me along the way - thank you.

A special note of appreciate to D. Musgrave and Jenna Brynes for hours of editing and critiquing, as well as friendship. You two have kept me grounded when I was lost in the clouds, and offered shoulders to cry on, when I needed it.

And to my husband - who supports me even when my characters scare him a little bit - my heartfelt thanks and love. Without him, these stories would never have been written.

TABLE OF CONTENTS:

MICHELLE
HOUSTON

TAMING THE WOLF

ANIMAL ATTRACTION

TAMING THE WOLF

"We've had another rogue incident." The words slammed into his brain over the phone line as Ben leaned back in his chair, clamping his eyes shut. He could remember all too vividly his own transition and the events that led up to it.

"How many were hurt?" Mindful of the fact that anyone could be listening in on the conversation, he chose his words carefully, avoiding the phrase that roared the back of his mind -- 'how many turned'.

"Three," came the long sigh on the other end of the line. The gritty voice deepened until Ben almost couldn't hear him with normal human senses. "We need your help. One must be sent to you. We don't have enough safe places for them all to go right now. Since you live in the middle of nowhere, you're his best bet."

Groaning silently to himself, Bed knew it wasn't a request. He was being politely ordered to put up the recently turned man, show him how to fight the urges to turn wolf, and how to exist with his world changed forever.

"When does he arrive?"

"He should be there about five. You must understand something Ben, if he can't handle it, you need to let us know. We can't risk people finding out what we are, even if it means taking an innocent his life."

Without saying anything Ben set the phone down in the cradle, knowing the conversation was over and didn't require his response. He had heard the same words once before, several years ago. The same man had spoken them to him, but at the time it was his life that hung in the balance. It had been made very clear to him that if he didn't control the beast beating at his insides every moment of the day, demanding its share of time, that he would be put down for the good of the race. Despite it being one of them going crazy that had turned him in the first place.

He wasn't sure what to expect, but when a tentative knock sounded on his door promptly at 5:00 pm that evening, he opened the door and got a good look at the man standing before him. For a brief moment, he could feel something inside of him and reaching out to the younger man.

There was something pushing the despair and fear aside in the younger man's gaze, a brief flicker of appreciation for Ben's toned body, his tanned skin, and crystal blue eyes. His nostrils flared with his every breath, the scent of pheromones pouring off him was unmistakable.

With shock, Ben acknowledged what his inner beast had understood, and embraced, almost instantaneously - the man standing before him was gay. Not in any stereotypical way, but there was no denying it. Nor was there any denying the arc of attraction flowing between them, as their gazes met.

Werewolves born of werewolves simply weren't often gay. Their biology didn't allow for it occur frequently in the population. But those turned, existed as they had before the bite--gay, straight, bisexual, and transsexual. It was

8

something Ben had come to accept; the likelihood of his ever finding a mate was extremely rare.

He couldn't help thinking that fact was another reason this young man was sent to him--for the chance there would be an attraction between them. He was sure the elders thought they could be potential mates. There was no telling what else had been factored into the decision. Only time would tell. Until then, he needed to get the younger man settled, fed, and begin testing and teaching him.

"Um, hi. I'm Nathan. The old guy, uh, Bryson said you'd help me understand what's going on."

Ben shook the hand that was held out to him, trying to ignore the bolt of lust that slammed through his body. He had a palpable sense that Nathan was going to be trouble, both in teaching Nathan how to control the beast within, and to his heart.

Three days later Ben was about at his wits end, his earlier guess that Nathan was trouble had long since been confirmed, on both counts. Nathan just wasn't getting it. He had tried everything Bryson had used with him--tossing him raw steak, causing the younger man to shift into his wolf being, and taunting him into a fight. Every time Nathan would lose control of his wolf's urge to assume the dominate role.

Ben was seriously worried he'd have to hide the younger man from Bryson to save his life, but doubted it would work for long and might cost them both their lives. Time was running short, and the more time he spent with Nathan the more he was coming to like him. The long dormant needs and desires had been awakened. The younger man had a quiet way about him, a gentleness that was completely at odds with his new life as a werewolf, but this dichotomy was infinitely attractive to the older man.

"I'm sorry Ben, I don't know what I'm doing wrong." Nathan slumped to the floor, his knees against his chest, his eyes liquid with misery. Ben could understand all too well what he was feeling. He had suffered the same thing a few years earlier. He had been out hiking when a wolf came out of nowhere. It had attacked him, viciously biting at his arms and legs as he struggled to get free. Then as he lay there, too weak to fight any more, and terrified he was dying, it had shifted to a man. Standing over him was a man with cold, dead eyes, and a cruel smile. On the ground, bleeding from multiple wounds, he had been unable to do more than lay there as the man turned and walked away, leaving him there to die.

Luckily for him Bryson, one of the elders, had been hunting the rogue and found him before he'd bled out. Bryson had taken him in and he and his mate cared for him, until Ben could do for himself. He had no real memory of the time between the two events, just a haze of pain and fear, of ripping the hair off of his body as he struggled to understand what was happening, and terror so deep it still swarmed over him just thinking about it.

Then the training had begun, four terrifying days where he struggled to control the beast, knowing what awaited him if he didn't. Finally, his fear of death won out, the anger at the hand fate had dealt him diminished, and he managed to put a leash on his inner wolf.

"It isn't that you're doing anything wrong, Nathan. It's simply that you believe your wolf self is stronger. You're defeated before you've even begun."

Crouching down, he looked Nathan directly in the eyes as he continued. "You know what's at stake here -- your life. You have to fight the wolf. It has to learn its place. If it continues to win, you die."

Nathan's gorgeous brown eyes closed at his words. Cupping the other man's chin in his hand Ben squeezed. "Look at me."

When Nathan's eyes opened, Ben comforted him. "I don't want it to happen, but if you can't learn to control the wolf they will kill you. And there won't be a damn thing I can do to stop it."

A wave of pain slammed at him at the realization that in a few more days if Nathan still wasn't in control of the wolf he would lose him. He had been alone so long, as the only werewolf he knew who longed for another man's touch, he now felt a spark of hope. Humans were out of bounds for their kind, too fragile to withstand the intensity of a werewolf's passion.

He wasn't even certain if during the heat of passion he could control his own wolf; he couldn't expose a potential human partner to the risk of injury or being turned, no matter how much he longed for someone to share his life.

He had started to grow close to Nathan, to feel a kinship that moved beyond the first spark of attraction into genuine fondness, and the hope that Nathan was his mate lingered at the back of his mind. He wasn't certain how to tell, but he knew when Bryson arrived to check things out that he could ask him then, if Nathan survived.

Despite the pressure they were both under, they had managed to steal quiet moments here and there to talk, to lean against the same tree, their bodies brushing lightly against each other as they talked about their pasts. It was a heady sensation for Ben, being able to talk to another person and have them understand what he was thinking, sometimes without have to vocalize it.

Nathan, he was coming to realize, was indeed a match for him. The younger man had a quiet peacefulness about him, a steady intelligence that Ben found ultra sexy. And the way he moved was seduction itself, made more so as the days rolled by and his body adjusted to the changes within it.

They had taken to running together, since they both shared a passion for it, their long legged strides a perfect match for each other. The one time Ben dared to let his wolf out to play, and had coaxed Nathan into doing the same, he found that they got along well even then. Nathan's was a smaller gray wolf, with a light coat. Ben's own wolf was a dark grey, with patches of black fur here and there.

Ben felt the first ripple rising to the surface, skin turning to fur, as his wolf felt him thinking about it, and was demanding its share of time. The last few days he hadn't allowed it control as much as normal and it was starting to get frustrated. Snarling, he regained his feet and stalked off, forcing the beast back. For Nathan's sake, he had to teach him control, then teach him how to partition his time between wolf and man.

Nathan moved to stand behind him, his hand light against his shoulder. "Ben?"

The question in his voice elicited a moan from Ben. It had been so long since a man had been this close to him, so long since he had felt the touch of another on his skin. He wanted it, craved the feel of two bodies sliding against each other in passion, of thrusting deep into another man's body and feeling him tense in pleasure. More than that though, he was coming to crave Nathan's touch; not just anyone would do anymore.

Ben flashed back to the previous day when he had provoked Nathan into a fight, had felt the pressure of the other man attempting to pin him down. Ben had almost given in to the sensations cascading over him and kissed the younger man, especially when he felt the press of Nathan's erection against his hip. Then he had felt the brush of fur against his skin as Nathan lost control of his body and the wolf worked its way to the surface. That fact allowed him the control he desperately needed.

"It's nothing you did Nathan. Nature is just kicking my ass at the moment."

The warmth of his touch shifted, as he slid his hand down Ben's back, lightly caressing him, trying to sooth as was his way. Tipping his chin to rest against his chest, Ben closed his eyes and fought the dueling sensations. Selfishly, he wanted to enjoy Nathan's touch, but by the same token he was denying the wolf the same courtesy. And it was biting and clawing at the injustice.

Butterfly soft, Nathan's lips pressed against his neck, the tentative touch more seductive than if he had unzipped his fly and sucked his cock into his mouth. The scent coming off him was different than his previous lovers; less intense, more seductive. Ben's body awakened with a roar, demanding all the things he had too long denied. He wanted to push Nathan away, to throw him to the ground and show him what happens when a wolf is tempted by what it cannot have.

Another kiss, this time on the soft skin of his bare shoulder where his tank top ended. Shivering at the intensity of his own needs, Ben finally won out over the wolf. With a whimper, it settled into the back of his mind, watching--waiting.

Turning in his arms, Ben met Nathan's gaze. Ben could feel the pace of the other man's heart increase, but he held himself motionless. Curious, he stroked his hand along Nathan's chest, brushing lightly over his nipples through the light cotton of his shirt. Fur rippled along Nathan's skin, appearing and disappearing where he stroked.

An idea formed in the back of his mind, a way to teach him control. It was risky, but if it worked would deepen the bond he was already feeling for the other man. With time quickly running out, he knew he had to start taking a more drastic approach. Nathan deserved his best efforts, deserved every chance at life, no matter how much they both might be hurt at the end of it.

Pulling back, he fought to control himself as he grasped Nathan's hand in his and led him down the hallway to his bedroom. The soft slap of the younger man's feet against the hardwood floors sent shivers down his spine and caused his wolf to snarl. They had been alone so long.

As he reached his room, he pushed the door open and pulled the other man inside, then closed the door. "Strip," Ben demanded as he moved toward the bed. Not waiting to see if he would obey, he crossed the room to his bed and pulled a length of white silk rope from the chest at the footboard. During the height of the full moon for the first few months Ben had bound himself to the bed, determined not to let the wolf get the better of him.

Once he had realized it wasn't the moon that called the wolf forth, but rather his own intense emotions that had allowed the animal inside to steal control, he packed it away. Now he made short work of wrapping it around the headboard, readying it for a man's wrist--for Nathan's wrists. Behind him he could hear the whisper of clothing being discarded and landing on the floor.

When he turned back around he paused at the beauty of the male form before him. Nathan was just shy of 25, and now that he had been turned, would age at a much slower rate. He was also in peak physical form, since the mutations magnified existing muscle, building it until he was easily three times stronger than a mortal male.

With a light dusting of brown hair on his chest, which thickened as his waist and narrowed into a seductive V that led all the way down to his erection, curling around the elongated shaft, highlighting the dusky skin, flushed with blood flow, he was perfect. Although his nose had been broken a time or two, and his features weren't the modern idea of masculine, his slim blade of a nose and high cheek bones gave him an aristocratic look.

His eyes were his best feature however, deep and dark, and filled with mysteries to be explored. Ben wanted to drown in them, to savor every moment that their gazes remained locked together. The steady tick of his bedside clock danced along the edge of his senses, reminding him there was a deeper purpose to their being together. That before the future could be considered, they both had to make it through the present.

"Lay down on the bed," Ben ordered, then cleared his throat at the deep rasp to his voice. He sounded like he hadn't spoken in months, when it reality it had been less than a few minutes. As Nathan moved to comply, Ben held out a loop of rope. As Nathan lay down on his back, and offered his slender wrist, Ben felt his chest tighten. The trust he could see in the younger man's eyes humbled him.

Even at his height of desperation he hadn't felt such for Bryson. He admired the elder, but had never trusted him blindly. Rather it has been the man's mate who had managed to get him through the worst of it, holding him late into the night, her dainty hands stroking through his hair as she whispered senseless words against his hair. The loss of control had been insidious, eating away at his self confidence, until she had conveyed some of her own feelings on the matter, making him feel less alone. Unlike her mate, she had also been turned traumatically. Bryson, for all the kind and decency within his soul, had been born of werewolves and knew nothing of the horror of having his life taken away, his very existence transformed into something he didn't recognize.

It was the memory of those moments, late in the night, held against a soft fragrant form that gave him the idea for how to help Nathan. The man was very obviously submissive, but the animal within him was not. Therefore he had to have a reason beyond him to stay in control, and Ben was going to give it to him. If it failed to work, he had no idea what else he could try.

Once the knot was tied around Nathan's right wrist, he moved around the bed, his right hand trailing down Nathan's form and back up as he went along, until he reached his other wrist. Like before, Nathan offered it without being asked, and without hesitation.

After tightening the rope, he moved back, settling at the foot of the bed at Nathan's feet. Picking up one of the younger man's feet, he ran his fingertips over the arch, just light enough to tickle. Nathan jerked, but didn't pull his foot away. "Here's how we are going to play this, Nathan. It's really very simple. You stay in control of the wolf, and I'll fuck you senseless." He paused for a moment and ran his fingertips up the other man's leg, brushing them gently along the back of his knee and trailed them back down again. "You let it take over, and I stop. Understand?"

He watched as the younger man licked his lips, his dark eyes wide with arousal and excitement. "Yes," he whispered his voice husky with sexual arousal. Ben allowed himself the pleasure of looking at the bound man, his pulse racing with the fact that the ropes were thick enough Nathan couldn't escape. He had the other man at his mercy, and he could do whatever he wanted to him.

Deciding to test Nathan's willpower he crawled over the younger man, straddling his lower legs, and leaned down, licking lightly at the rapidly darkening tip of his cock. Nathan bucked on the bed, his slender hips jerking as Ben took him deep into his mouth, sucking as hard as he could before suddenly stopping. His gaze roved over skin, seeking out patches of fur.

Finding none, he pulled back and kissed along Nathan's legs, the dusting of hair tickling his clean-shaven face. Moving slowly upward, he shifted so that he straddled Nathan's waist, the crotch of his shorts rubbing deliciously against the other man's cock, tormenting them both.

Bracing himself with his hands next to Nathan's head, he leaned down and pressed his lips against Nathan's, thrusting his tongue deep as the dewy softness of the other man's lips parted for him, eagerly welcoming the deepening of the kiss. As their tongues mated, he rubbed his groin slowly against the other man's, drawing forth soft moans from deep within his chest. Ben could feel Nathan's gasps flowing into his mouth, and he increased the pressure, until he had to throw back his own head and groan. It had been so damn long.

With a muffled curse, he climbed off Nathan and stood beside the bed. Looking down at the man spread out so deliciously before him, he had to fight back his own wolf again. His hands unsteady, he unzipped his pants and pulled his cock out, slowly stroking his fist over the aching head, enfolding the shaft in a tight grip. Nathan's gaze locked on the movements of his hands as he slowly stroked up and down, bringing some relief to the pressure, but at the same time making it more intense when he stopped.

Needing more, Ben tossed his clothes aside and opened the drawer on his bedside table. Pulling out his favorite lubricant, he coated his cock liberally, his movements just slow enough to torment.

Satisfied he had covered himself well, he moved to the foot of the bed and knelt between Nathan's legs. "Pull your legs up," he ordered, uncertain what he would do if Nathan didn't comply. It was with relief he watched as Nathan slowly folded his legs back against his chest, the long expanse of muscle framing his cock, his puckered butt-ring flaring as the muscles surrounding it flexed.

Looking over the other man, Ben made certain he didn't see any hint of the wolf was taking over. He shifted so he lay down over Nathan, his arms cupped against the backs of the younger man's knees, holding his legs pinned against his chest. Carefully, he nudged his cock head against the tantalizing ring of the other man's asshole and pressed gently forward.

Nathan growled in response, the pupils of his eyes dilating and shifting, becoming more wolf than man.

"Control the wolf, or I stop," Ben growled.

Nathan gave a jerk of his head and closed his eyes, his breath coming in panting gasps as Ben pressed forward, his cock slipping a bit into the warmth of the other man's ass.

"Look at me," he demanded, waiting until he could see Nathan's eyes had returned to normal before thrusting forward, drawing a howl from the younger man. Looking into the brown depths of Nathan's eyes, Ben started to lose himself as he lunged forward, driving his cock deep into the warm recesses of the other man before pulling back.

Conscious of the feel of the other man's skin, he struggled to stay in control of his own wolf as he began the mating dance, thrusting forward and claiming what was his, then pulling back, only to thrust in again. Beneath him Nathan groaned and whimpered as he worked them both into a state of frenzied need, drawing it out as long as possible.

Dipping his head, he nipped at Nathan's full lower lip, just enough to slightly sting, then thrust his tongue past his parted lips. His own balls tight with the imminent orgasm, he continued thrusting his hips, pounding into Nathan's welcoming heat.

Ben broke the kiss as warm drops of moisture brushed against his stomach with each intimate movement. Pulling back, he sat up just enough to watch the liquid seep from the slit in Nathan's cock as he increased the pace of his thrusts. The cords of the brunette's neck stood out as he tried to arch into the motions, impaling himself harder and deeper on Ben's cock.

Grasping Nathan's ankles, Ben lifted them to rest on his shoulders and shifted his hold to Nathan's hips, pulling him down and into each thrust, his balls slamming against the other man's ass-cheeks with the force of his thrusts. The scent of their desire seeped from their pores, mingling together, the pheromones coating them both. Ben could feel his wolf clawing at his insides, howling for its mate.

"Oh…God…Ben, I can't control it," Nathan gasped out as his pupils dilated.

Ben could only guess that Nathan was struggling as much as he was, but he was winning. "You give in and I stop," he gritted out, not knowing how the hell he would accomplish his threat. Stopping now would kill him, it felt so right to be deep within Nathan's ass, to be so intimately close to a man he was coming to feel he could easily love.

The past few days Nathan had shown warmth of character and an ability to laugh at himself that was self deprecating, but in a charming way. Being this close to him, feeling his body quiver with passion, smelling the echo of desire on every inch of his skin, was more than Ben had ever hoped to find.

Nathan struggled with his bonds, his wrists twisting wildly. "I need my hands free," he gasped out, his body tightening with a hint of panic.

Despite his better judgment, Ben pulled back and quickly undid the knots, freeing Nathan. Immediately the younger man reached out to him, wrapping his arms around Ben's neck and pulling him down against his body, draping his legs over Ben's arms and spreading them wide enough to accommodate his frame..

The heat radiating from Nathan was an aphrodisiac all its own. Slowing his pace, Ben gently thrust forward and glided back out, his cock barely moving at all. In response, Nathan squeezed his muscles, increasing the pleasurable pain of being held within such a tight cavity.

Ben growled as his wolf echoed enjoyment of the sensation, clawing at his insides. Shuddering at the dual sensations, of working in concert with the wolf for their mutual pleasure, he closed his eyes and kissed Nathan, drawing out the tongue play until he couldn't contain himself any more. Picking up the pace of his thrusts, he drove harder and deeper into the other mans' ass, feeling the stream of his lover's pre-come against his stomach.

"Mine," Ben growled, determined to place his claim on the other man, to mark him before the council arrived to check things out. Even if Nathan couldn't fully control his wolf, he wasn't going to let anything happen to him. If need be, Ben was willing to take personal responsibility for the other man, knowing if he screwed up and lost control both their lives would be forfeit. "Say it!" he ordered Nathan.

He couldn't lose Nathan.

"I'm yours," Nathan gasped out, his ass ring squeezed hard enough to make Ben groan.

"Say it again."

"I'm yours Ben, ah God, I'm yours!"

Nathan started moaning, his voice deepening beyond the realm of human hearing as he whimpered his need, whispering words that only inflamed Ben's need to claim him. Feeling his chest tighten with emotion, the wolf inside howling at the idea of its mate being taken away, he pushed himself harder, pumping his hips more aggressively than he would with a mortal, and Nathan met him thrust for thrust.

The warm pool of moisture between them expanded as Nathan let out a howl, his body bunking and thrashing as an orgasm washed over him. Ben growled and thrust hard and deep, then held himself motionless as Nathan's ass clenched around his cock, drawing his own climax from him.

Panting, he held himself above the younger man, determined not to make him feel trapped as his breathing slowly returned to normal and he could think again. Opening his eyes, he met startled brown eyes that thankfully didn't hold a hint of the wolf within.

"You ok?" he managed to gasp out, wondering as he said it how he had pulled together enough coherent thought after such a mind-blowing and pivotal event. At the moment of his orgasm he had felt Nathan's pleasure echoing within him. There was nothing before in his life that could have prepared him to feel the dual sensations of impaling and being impaled, of his own orgasm squared, of the tenderness and need to submit melding with the demand of domination. He could see the same confusion echoed within his lover's brown eyes.

"Yeah, oh man yeah." Nathan replied.

Pulling free of his lover's ass, Ben rolled to the side and pulled Nathan against him, pressing soft kisses against the other man's bite stung lips. He couldn't remember biting Nathan's lip as his passion rose, in fact he couldn't remember breaking the kiss and pulling back, but knew he had.

"What just happened?" Nathan asked with a searching look in his eyes.

As much as Ben wanted to be able to explain it to the other man, he hadn't a clue himself, and had to tell him such. "I wished I knew." Stroking his hand over his lover's back, Ben resisted the urge to latch on tightly to him, to hold him close enough he could curl up inside the younger man. "But we can ask Bryson when he arrives in a few days. I'm sure he'll know."

Nathan tensed in his arms at the mentioned of the elder's name.

"Relax, it'll be ok. You did wonderful controlling the wolf, and we have time to work on the rest."

"I didn't though, not after the beginning anyways. It stayed alongside me and stopped fighting me. In fact, I could hear its howl of pleasure ringing in my ears when I came."

Ben continued to stroke his hands over Nathan's sweaty skin, loving the feel of its texture under his fingertips. There was something soothing about holding the other man close and breathing in his scent. His mind was busy turning over the facts. He and Nathan had shared each other's pleasure, and it seemed both their wolves had shared things within them.

Two days later, he was still trying to figure things out. The second and third time he had made love to Nathan events had gone the same as before. The wolves stayed under control, and seemed to experience things alongside them. They had also shared the last moments of orgasm with each other. Thankfully Nathan had learned to control the wolf under other circumstances, and had successfully let it out to play, then harnessed it again several times.

The sound of a car pulling into the drive pulled Ben out of his thoughts and back to the present. Standing quickly, he moved across the room where Nathan sat frozen in his chair, tension radiating from him. "It'll be ok," he soothed as he grasped the younger man's shoulder, and giving him a squeeze.

As a knock sounded at the door, Ben reluctantly moved to answer it. As Bryson entered the room the tension level went up noticeably and Nathan stood, his shoulders squared. Ben felt pride for his lover; he was facing down his fears head on. Despite their short acquaintance, he knew Nathan was someone he wanted to consider the possibilities with. Already he was growing used to falling asleep with the brunette man in his arms, of waking up holding him tight.

"Welcome to my home, Bryson."

"My thanks," the elder tipped his head in a brief nod, reminding Ben of royalty. The aristocratic features and regal bearing only helped the image.

"Would you like to sit down?"

"No, my friend, I'll only interrupt your day for a few moments. Has Nathan learned control?"

Ben could feel Nathan trembling and reached out to clasp his hand, not caring what Bryson thought. It was better he knew ahead of time that Ben was attached to him. "Yes, I believe he has."

Without a response, Bryson shifted into his wolf form. He did it so smoothly, Ben didn't see it coming. Bryson lunged at Nathan, causing him let go of Ben's and backed up. His eyes were wide in fear and he threw his hands up in defense, stepping back further, trying to get away. Just before he reached Nathan, Bryson shifted back into his human form.

Ben understood instantly--he was testing Nathan. Unlike his own test where he had been forced into anger, Nathan had to prove he had control of his fear.

Nathan had confessed to Ben his turning. He had been transformed by a vicious surprise attack, and in the dark of the night. The out pouring of Nathan's fear as he told Ben of the attack pressed tight against Ben's chest. After his own attack, Ben had been angry--angry at being robbed of his life, of his feelings of helplessness. For the more submissive man, the fear of the unknown ruled him, and allowed his wolf a window to seize control.

Now they could form a relationship, a mutual sharing of the body that both inhabited.

"I'm sorry for scaring you Nathan, but unfortunately it had to be done. I wish you to know I would never hurt you. You are a victim of circumstances, and I am thrilled to see you overcoming them."

Nathan moved to stand next to Ben and nodded, his motions a quick jerk of his head. Ben met the other man's gaze and could still see the whites of his eyes, but the panic was slowly receding.

"Is there anything I can answer while I am here?"

Ben wanted to ask, but didn't know the outcome it would have if he did. He spoke quickly, almost in a rush to force the words out before he could change his mind. "When I made love to Nathan our minds connected and I could feel what he was feeling."

The smile that lit Bryson's face was dazzling. For a moment, Ben could feel himself dazzled by the elder, but the brush of Nathan against his side ended it.

"I had hoped when I sent him to you that this would happen. It's a mate bond, and it will deepen over time, until you are two halves of the same whole, complete within yourself, in harmony with the wolf, and with each other. In your case, we never knew if it would happen, even if another gay werewolf were found. It seems his turning did have a bigger purpose. Is that all?"

Ben nodded and said goodbye to his mentor and friend.

Nathan grasped his hand and held on tight, the warmth of his touch a comfort as Bryson gave a final nod and turned for the door. After opening it, he glanced back. "If ever you need me--"

Ben nodded in understanding. As the door closed behind Bryson, he pulled Nathan into his arms and kissed him, his wolf growling in encouragement as the desire to claim his lover welled with him.

MICHELLE HOUSTON

EMBRACING THE LEOPARD

ANIMAL ATTRACTION

EMBRACING THE LEOPARD

Erik braced his elbows on his knees and looked out over the lake, enjoying the serenity of the setting sun, and the steady call of the cicadas and crickets around him, as they courted potential mates. Breathing in deeply the sweet spring scents, he felt at peace for the first time in more than a week.

Visiting his family, his pack, was always hard. Seeing his sisters and brothers happily mated, playing with the various nephews and nieces, being the favorite uncle, was a bittersweet delight. All too soon, the conversations inevitably turned to his finding a mate, and then an uncomfortable hush would fall. He was an outcast, without being one. His family tried to understand him, tried to accept that he didn't want a female in his life, that the longing was for the strong arms of another man, but they just couldn't.

The percentage of gay shifters was marginal; the likelihood of finding a mate was slim.

So he would begin to pull back, to spend more time with the cubs and less with the adults, and then he would one evening quietly slip away. It hurt, seeing all of the eligible males, and knowing that none of them were for him. With the faint stirrings that heralded the beginning of the mating urge, it had grown worse.

The wind picked up, ruffling through his brown hair, sending it curling in his eyes. Dipping his chin, he blew it off of his face, and turned his gaze back to the ripples the breeze made on the water.

A flash of movement in the stillness of the night caught his attention, and turning his head slightly he tracked the movement of a young leopard as it crept slowly towards the lake. Breathing deeply, he caught the briefest whiff of its scent, and a frown curled his lips. It wasn't fully a cat. Inhaling again as the wind picked up, he managed to catch just enough to know it was a shifter. Something about the scent teased at his memory, but the markings weren't any he recognized. Unlike some packs, all of his had a lighter, mottled yellow and black coloring. This leopard had the dark golden coat, the swirling rosettes barely noticeable in the fading light. Growling silently, he fought the urge to shift and force the intruder out of his territory, even as he admired the beauty of its motions.

With the wind current on his side, he was content to sit back and watch the leopard, for the moment, to judge the threat he possessed. Highly territorial by nature, he was also lonely, and if the other shifter didn't pose a threat, he might consider allowing it to skirt his territory in return for companionship.

Unlike their animal counterparts, leopard shifters craved interaction with each other, needing to feel the touch of another shifter to retain control over their animal counterpart. Which was why being away from his pack was so hard -- Erik craved touch, but had to deny himself.

As the leopard reached the water's edge, a shimmer of mist wrapped around it and then in its place an adult male human stood, his dark skin glistening like finely polished ebony in the moonlight. Erik watched silently as a breeze ruffled the man's dark locks, sending the shoulder length hair riding the air currents, while the male removed him clothing. Every time Erik watched another of his kind shift, it always amazed him that somehow, the process knew what molecules were the shifter and what was clothing, and everything went back together properly.

The water rippled around the other shifter as he stepped nude into the lake, and with a sudden explosion of motion he dived into the warm water, his form cutting a smooth line through the still waters.

Content for the moment, Erik admired the male's form as he rapidly put distance between himself and the shore, then suddenly dove under the water, only to surface again almost twenty feet from where he had been. As the unknown male started back toward him and reached the shore, the air currents shifted slightly and he could see the instant his scent reached the other man's nose.

He quickly grabbed his clothes and started pulling them on, while he scanned the area around him with a piercing gaze. Leisurely, Erik stood and worked his way down the slope of the hill he had rested upon. The closer he got the more agitated the other man's motions were. Slowing his pace, he allowed him time to dress, timing his arrival at the water's edge to the zipping of the man's jeans.

"Nice night for a swim," he drawled, a teasing note purposefully injected into his voice. He wanted to put the other man at ease for some reason.

"I'll leave." The other shifter held up his hands in front of his chest, palms facing outwards, fingers uncurled. He started to step sideways, moving to edge his way around and slip back into the night. Erik stalled his motions by stepped back himself, assuming a relaxed, non-threatening posture.

"I have no problem with you my friend," he responded, pitching his voice lower and drawing his words out in a soothing manner. "You respect this area, and me, and we will continue to not have any problems." A hesitant jerky nod was his answer.

"I'm Erik, and you are?"

"Brandon. I didn't know this was pack land."

"Indeed, it isn't. This land isn't pack land, it's privately owned." Although they hadn't yet determined a hierarchy between them, since the land they were on was Erik's, his word was law.

"Ah." Brandon's stance relaxed. Trespassing on private land was one thing, pack land a totally different issue. The scent markers for pack land were generally more obvious, and the penalties harsher. Erik had purposefully not marked his land beyond the house area, wanting to encourage wildlife to visit. The scent of leopard would scare many of them off.

"Finish your swim if you wish. I don't mind."

Brandon shrugged, the rise and fall of his shoulders drawing Erik's attention. The wind shifted directions again, masking his scent but pushing the other man's toward him. The faintest wisps of curious arousal teased his nose. Allowing his gaze to trail over the other man, slowing perusing the lines and curves of his body, he waited to see if there was any reaction. The silence stretched between them, then Brandon slowly grabbed the edge of his T-shirt and pulled it over his head.

The briefest of smiles curled his lips, a dare implied by the twinkle in his eyes. He was pushing Erik's inner beast, but it was the smell of Brandon's building arousal that was torturing him. It had been so long since he had been around another male who shared his interest in men. Only once had he come across another shifter who unquestionably preferred men, and he was already mated, thus out of his reach.

"I was thinking to camp here tonight, so if you have any suggestions for a good camping spot that's out of the way, I'd love to hear them." As he spoke his hands went to the top of his jeans and started unzipping them. The button had never managed to be slid through its hole when he had hurried to dress earlier.

Erik pushed his leopard to the back of his soul as he watched the other man strip. Unlike the hurried movements of before, this was almost a strip tease. All that was missing was the loud music and the presence of other men clamoring for Brandon's attention.

Growling softly at the idea of sharing the shifter with other men, Erik yanked his shirt off, sending buttons flying. The smile on Brandon's lips grew wider in response, and the scent on the air currents subtly changed. Judging by the change, and his facial expression, Erik gathered he liked the forcefulness of his motions. His motions slowed, turned almost teasing as he finished undressing. The backs of his hands brushed against his nipples, tightening the buds into tiny black pearls that stood out proud against rich dark skin.

Erik's knees almost wouldn't hold his weight at the sight. Clearing his throat, he worked to get the words out. "You can stay here tonight. As I said before, respect me and the land, and we won't have any problems."

Most shifters he had run across already had a deep-seated respect for the environment, but there had been a few who had lost their way, and no longer walked the path of harmony with the planet. He didn't understand it, and accepted he probably never would.

"That won't be a problem," Brandon responded as he shimmied out of his pants, dragging his boxers down with them. The damp cloth attempted to cling, making for an interesting show as his moved, his cock jiggling with the motions, drawing Erik's gaze. He was almost hypnotized by the soft swaying of the organ, the black curls surrounding the base neatly trimmed to allow the best access.

Yet there was that teasing of his memory with each inhalation. The scent coming off of the other man was heady in its rush of pheromones, but also gave him the impression that he knew the other shifter somehow. But that was impossible.

Rather than step forward and press against the other man, as his raging hormones were demanding he do, Erik slowed his pace and allowed his clothing to fall from his body, rather than push it off. Brandon was already back in the water and leisurely swimming around when Erik was naked, his own cock hard and demanding attention.

Stepping in the water warmed by the earth and sun, he tipped forward and sent himself in the opposite direction of the younger shifter, wanting to see if he would respond, or simply go his own way.

A playful tug on his ankle was his answer moments before he was dragged downward. Inhaling a last quick breath, he dropped below the surface, the water rushing over him. Holding the air tight in his lungs he doubled his body over, and grabbed at the other man's shoulder. Their wet bodies slid against each other, and Brandon pressed close against him, then leaned down and joined their mouths together.

Exhaling slightly into the other man's mouth as he parted his lips for a kiss, Erik clasped only Brandon's hips and pulled their groins tightly together. Blood hardened flesh rubbed together, tormenting them both as they kissed underwater until desperate for air, Erik broke free and surged for the surface.

As he cleared the water, Erik opened his eyes and stared into playful blue ones, so at odds within a dark face, which triggered a memory. Almost ten years before he had frolicked in the water with several male shifters, particularly one ornery young man, a teen barely able to control his quickly growing body. He resembled a newborn fawn more than a nearly adult cat.

Brandon smiled and Erik knew in that moment his mind wasn't playing tricks on him. The youngest son of the alpha of his uncle's pack, the man standing in the warm water before him, was that young shifter.

At the cusp of adulthood, his body turning from teen to man, he had been attractive. Now he was breathtaking, the leashed power of his form, the barely controlled animal within. His long hair curled around his shoulders, his chest hair curled into a matt against sculpted muscles, and narrowed into a V which drew Erik's eyes down his body.

"I wondered if you would remember me."

Erik blinked, uncertain just how to respond to that. Thinking the other shifter was a stranger, someone he could have a passing relationship with and let him drift out of his life was one thing. The possibility of constantly running into Brandon, wanting more than a young cat not yet in the heat of the mating need could give was something completely different. Without the intense pheromones, there was no guarantee that they would bond for life.

"What exactly was your plan for this evening?"

Brandon shrugged, sending his long hair cascading down his chest, the water beading and rolling down tightly packed muscles. Erik wanted badly to follow its path with his tongue, but knew he couldn't. Not now, not knowing who Brandon was.

"I originally did plan to just camp out. But when I saw you standing there, still the same man who played so carefree with me years ago, still as intoxicating as you were then, I decided to see what could come of it."

"Come of what?"

Brandon laughed softly, the sound music to Erik's deprived ears. Living alone voluntarily didn't mean he had to like it. As he grew older, the need for someone in his life was growing. Despite craving the touch of another man rather than a woman, the mating urge was upon him, his body demanding he claim another as his own.

Unfortunately, there weren't any others to be had among his pack, and being around unmated males that didn't follow his persuasion was torture. The need, the deep yearning, the hope that one day one of them would start sending out pheromones that would call to him, was sheer hell.

The knowing it probably would never happen was worse. Erik had a feeling a passing fling, without the hope of a future, combined with constantly having to run into Brandon, knowing what he had had, but wouldn't again, would send him over the edge.

"You're gay. I'm gay. I knew then that I was attracted to you, but I was ordered to leave you alone, at least until I was deemed an adult. I waited ten years, every night wondering if I would approach you, finally an adult, and find that you had found someone. Wondering if I would approach you and the chemistry wouldn't be there. But now I know."

Sons of cat alphas generally were alphas themselves, and at the steel lacing Brandon's words, Erik had no doubt that the man standing before him would soon come into his legacy and start gathering young shifters to himself, and lead them, forming his own pack.

Brandon inhaled deeply, his eyes turning indigo as his nostrils flared. Looking down, Erik could see the other man's cock hardening further, the muscles of his stomach rigid.

"Your need is upon you." If anything his smile grew wider, more calculating as his gaze trailed over Erik's body. Feeling a flush of warmth at the other man's attention, he forced himself not to back away. It was his kind's way when challenged, and although he was a beta facing a future alpha, he wasn't about to back down from one who hadn't come into his own yet. Alphas had to prove themselves, and Erik had already shown himself to be a strong beta, one of his packs fiercest warriors. Years in the military had only enhanced his natural instincts, until only his bare nature kept him from taking that step into alpha territory.

Brandon on the other hand was only a few steps into adulthood, without a pack of his own, and without rank beyond the alpha's son within his father's.

Brandon stepped closer, the water level lowering to just below his heavy ball-sac, jostling the tempting flesh with every lap of the lake against the shore. Reaching out, he cupped his hand over Erik's cock, slowing stroking down the length. Getting a firm grip he pulled Erik forward until their bodies were pressed together, their skin still slick with the coating of water.

"Males of my family experience their need early, often just after reaching adulthood. Many of the elders think it comes from being a long line of alphas, with several born each generation, and needing to find a mate quickly to start our own pack." As he talked, Brandon backed Erik slowly out of the water until they stood together just on the shore. "Regardless, I can already feel its call coursing through me, which is why I am here tonight. I needed to get away from everyone, or go insane."

Erik understood completely what the other male was saying. It had often been the same for him, driving him to a solitude he really didn't want. His nature longed for pack, the leopard within demanding the touch of others of his kind, the familiar blending of scents that spelled out a family.

But each moment with the pack was torture, slowly seeping the humanity out of him, until he couldn't handle being around his own kind, as much as he craved it.

Brandon leaned down and nipped at the side of Erik's neck. Holding himself motionless as the intoxicating need to mate threatening to overwhelm him, was agony for Erik. Struggling to stay clearheaded when all he wanted to do was drag the younger shifter to the ground and mate with him was hard, but he managed it somehow.

"I wanted you, even then." Erik shivered at the vivid imagery filling his mind. When he had first met the younger man, Brandon had just turned 18. Lanky and tall,

34

his body had shimmered with the droplets of water clinging to him, just as he was now. Erik had wanted him even then, but the decade difference between them was too large. Brandon seemed to echo his need. "I was too young to claim you. Now I'm not."

Without any warning he swept his leg behind Erik and dropped him to the ground, falling down on top of him.

"I'm done waiting."

Stunned as the breath rushed out of his mouth, he unconsciously allowed Brandon's questing tongue past his parted lips. As reason returned with a swift inhalation through his nose, he cupped his hands on the back of the shifter's head and gave in to the need coursing through him.

The pheromones Brandon was putting off mingled with his own, and nature claimed them both. There was no denying the need that rushed between them. The attraction was too strong, and the demands of the mating need were riding them both too hard.

Thankfully, somehow their bodies always knew their own mate, often before the mind had a chance to catch up. Despite not knowing the details of Brandon's life, Erik could feel instinctively enough about his character, could almost hear the molecules of his being embracing who and what Brandon was.

Brandon shifted against him, rubbing his hard cock against Erik's stomach, leaving a faint trail of pre-come mixed with his scent markers. Trailing a leisurely path, he glided downward, his cock rubbing along Erik's thighs, then back up until a tiny pool of come formed on Erik's chest. Straddling the prone man, he sat up and while Erik watched him, enjoying the feel of his touch, Brandon rubbed his hands over the older shifter's chest, marking his territory with the strongest of his scents.

His hands sure and firm, Brandon grasped Erik's cock and stroked up and down, coaxing a steady stream of pre-come from the tip until it coated his palms, then he started rubbing it over his own body. Almost clumsily as the seriousness of his actions warred at the back of his mind with the needs of his body, Erik helped rub his own scent into the other man's skin.

The light breeze wafted over them, carrying the mingling scent of their bodies to Erik's nose and his nostrils flared as a surge of need slammed against him. He wanted to be mated; his body was no longer content to wait as the leopard within roared out its need.

He could feel the fur rippling along his arms and chest as the animal savagely demanded its dues. Held in check too long, it had found a mate and it wasn't willing to be denied, even if it meant his human mind hadn't had a chance to catch up yet to his animal heart.

As Brandon leaned down and gripped the skin at the base of Erik's neck in his teeth, Erik tipped his head back, allowing his access. "You know what you're doing can't be undone," he panted, wanting to make certain the newly turned adult understood the severity of his actions. He was marking Erik, staking a claim to him, and in turn, he was marking himself as well.

"Yes," Brandon purred against his neck then he bit down, drawing the briefest trickle of blood. He pressed the side of his neck against Erik's lips, and he reciprocated, allowing a few drops of the alphas blood to coat his tongue, the scent forever marked in his brain.

He could now track the younger man, and he could be tracked, allowing them both the ability to protect and be protected by their mate. The leopard roared its satisfaction and surged again against his skin, and for a brief moment Erik allowed it to surface, savoring the feel of his body contorting into his animal form, before he leashed it again.

His memories of the first time they had met, ten years before, overlaid with the man who faced him now. It was a heady realization that in some way he had known it was coming, had hoped and prayed for it, even as he denied himself that hope, and turned away from his kind. It was simply too painful.

Now, he could embrace his feeling, as he embraced the younger alpha in his arms. His need to submit warred with his need to demand his mating dues. The long suppressed need won.

Growling his need through vocal cords no longer fully human, he bucked against Brandon, his cock throbbing, almost painfully, as his ass tightened in anticipation of the claiming to come.

An answering growl sounded above him as with a smooth motion Brandon shifted back, grabbed his hip and rolled him over. Erik barely managed to shift himself to his hands and knees before Brandon was pulling him back against him, his cock sliding into the cleft of Erik's ass.

Brandon rocked against him, his erection sliding up and down, leaving a wet trail and covering Erik's skin in his scent. His hands clasped Erik's hips, pulling him tight against his body, molding his chest against Erik's back as he hunched over him, and mounted him, his cock nudging at the entrance to his ass. Relaxing, even as anticipation flooded him, Erik offered the puckered ring for his lover's claiming.

Erik surged over him, his cock slipping past the sphincter and driving home, hard and fast. Tears of pain sprung to life in Erik's eyes even as he arched backward, driving Brandon's cock deeper into his body, allowing him to claim him, to reach the animal growling deep within. The pain receded as his nerve endings flared to life, enjoying the glide of Brandon's cock as he thrust forward, shifted back, then thrust again, the steady stream of his pre-come easing his motions.

His cock so hard it curled upwards against his stomach despite his position, Erik growled for more, beyond the ability to speak. He was a creature of sensation, the leopard inside taking over his mind as it greeted its mate, submitting and demanding at the same time.

It welcomed the feel of his alpha covering him, tightening his ass-ring around the other man's cock. Closing his eyes, Erik surrendered himself to the mating dance, feeling the scent of the other man seeping into his pores.

The light breeze swirled over his skin, sending shivers down his spine as the water of his skin dried, the chill contrasting with the heat of his lover's skin. There was no denying it, the moment Brandon's cock slid past the tight ring of his ass, they were lovers, mates, partners.

Arching his back, he allowed the leopard to rise to the surface, just barely keeping it leashed as fur rippled over his skin and Brandon drove harder into his ass. The sound of skin slapping against skin echoed in the still night. Around them the other creatures fell silent, and it was as if the lovers were the only ones that existed.

Panting with the need riding him, Erik growled with each exhalation, his balls tightening, his cock aching for release. As if Brandon knew how hard he was struggling to not surrender to his orgasm, a warm fist wrapped around his cock, squeezing tight and holding back the waves that threatened to swarm over him.

Erik breathed a sigh of relief as he tightened his anus, holding his lover's erection deep inside. He could hold out, he wouldn't embarrass himself like a randy youth and orgasm too early. At least he thought he could hold back until the fist gripping him relaxed and started to slide up and down his length.

As the pace of the cock in his ass matched the steady rhythm, he closed his eyes and let the inevitable wash over him. Jerking his hips against the hand holding him, he climaxed, his come covering Brandon's fingers and splattering his stomach. Teeth nipped at his neck, and Erik spread his legs wider, lowering himself closer to the ground and giving his lover a freer range of motions.

Brandon shifted the hand from Erik's cock to his hip, and holding him gripped tightly, started pounding into him, the force of the motions almost savage, and Erik's leopard roared its approval. His eyes flew open as his cock started to harden again, the deep scents coming off of Brandon an instant aphrodisiac. Fur rippled down his back and the sights of the forest took on a new intensity as his eyes changed. A growl sounded in his ear as Brandon struggled with his own leopard.

The mating scent deepened, until every breath he took blended them more and more, until Erik wasn't certain he could tell anymore where he ended and Brandon began. Tipping his head back against his lover's firm shoulder, he opened him mouth and was rewarded by Brandon's lips covering his, his tongue sweeping past his parted lips and into his mouth.

His pace of the cock impaling him slowed, until they were rocking together in place. He could feel every breath Brandon took, both against his back and his cheek. His own breathing was rapid as he fought the urge to come again, when Brandon, despite his younger years, was still hard and throbbing in his ass.

Breaking the kiss, Brandon let loose a growl of his own, and Erik's heart started racing. Closing his eyes, he welcomed the fast pace the younger man set as he started thrusting hard and fast into his ass. As Brandon started to growl and grunt, Erik tried to make out what he was repeating, even as his mind said it didn't care, and surrendered to the demands of his body.

At the feel of Brandon's cock jerking inside of him, the warmth of his come flooding his ass, he shouted the same words again, and Erik could finally make it out. "My mate. Mine!"

Feeling like lightening had just jolted his balls, Erik jerked as his own orgasm crashed, sending a steady trickle of come from his cock-slit. He collapsed against the ground, Brandon's weight coming down on top of him. Erik moaned softly as Brandon pulled back and rolled to his side. His body protested the loss of his lover's warmth, the loss of the erection joining them together, even as his leopard purred in satisfaction at finding its mate.

Feeling conflicted at having given himself so completely to a man he didn't know well, yet thrilled at having found his mate, he simply savored the moment. Rolling into his side, he curled up against Brandon's side. Brandon opened his arms and pulled him closer, settling him against his chest, guiding one of Erik's legs to rest between his own, their groins tight together.

As the sun rose over the hastily erected tent, Erik curled tighter against Brandon's chest, the feel of a hand stroking up and down his back strange, yet comforting. After their intense mating of the night before, he and Brandon had decided to set up a camp site and sleep under the stars, rather than inside of his house. Together they had put up the tent before crawling inside and giving in to the desire arching between then again.

They had also spent a good deal of time talking, about their hopes and dreams, their plans for the future. Brandon had already started to form the basis of his own pack, slowly cultivating members of his generation, as well as elders. Erik knew of at least three of his own pack that would probably follow him, since he was an alpha's mate, and thus a pack leader.

That was how packs were born, not of challenges for dominance, but with ties to existing packs, cultivating alliances and staking their own territory. With the threats that faced them if their existence was ever found out, most of the alphas knew what was at stake.

Now, his leopard sleeping deep inside of him, Erik found his mind able to reason through things. Feeling the warmth of Brandon's body, he felt at home for the first time in a long while. Already he felt like he had known Brandon for years, rather than only twice, with a ten year spread. That week he had spent with the young alpha, over a decade before, was still a fond and vivid memory, but was slowly being eclipsed by the reality of the man he had become.

Because they had spent the night alternating between talking, and mating, now his body was blissfully lethargic, the mating need a muted whisper, and he was ready to surrender to sleep.

"I think we should stay here." Brandon's words startled him, and the fog of sleep lifted as they sank in. He had expected as alpha that his lover would want to find his own territory, not setting into another man's. He should have known that Brandon would want to stay close to where they had committed themselves to each other. The sentimentality that rested at the core of the other man had already started to be apparent.

Erik knew his pack would welcome the other man as an alpha in his own right, and a neutral line would be forged between the territories. With a soft nod, Erik curled tighter into Brandon's frame and savored every moment of being held. For the first time in a long time, he felt hope-- he would have pack in his life again, and a strong lover in his bed.

UNLEASHING THE JAGUAR

For the hundredth time, Michael cursed himself for being seven kinds of a fool as he paced the length of his cage. The sounds of the zoo settled into a nighttime rhythm as the last of the attendants left, leaving the animals alone for the night with just a few guards.

During the day he tried to ignore his situation, preferring to nap and avoid looking at all of the people who embraced their freedom without even being truly aware of it. They had no idea, thinking about their job and family lives as being trapped, but at any moment they could walk away. He had once felt the same way, feeling trapped by his nature, frustrated that he couldn't allow himself to shift when his beast felt like it. Instead he had to keep it on a tight chain, forcing half of his soul into a dormant state unless the situation was right.

Now trapped in his jaguar form and in a zoo, he knew what true enslavement felt like. The complete loss of will, the inability to change a damn thing about his situation, without damning thousands of his kind to potential extermination was a heavy burden to bear. Almost as heavy as the loss of his mate.

Growling his frustration, he tried to figure a way out of the cage. As a jaguar, he couldn't open the cage door; there was no way he could as a human. Worse, he couldn't risk the chaos that would ensue if he were caught on camera shifting, so that he could try to escape. Flopping down on the cool ground, he laid his head on his front legs and huffed out a sigh.

There was no way out.

For the rest of his life he was stuck in his animal form, and behind bars. Thankfully the zoo hadn't brought in a mate for him yet. As much as he got along with his animal kin, there was no way he was going to be mating with a non-shifter jaguar. The very idea repulsed; despite his animal nature, true jaguars were non-sentient at a human level.

Which meant that in addition to being trapped in a cage, he would be alone. Having thought himself alone after Danny left, he hadn't realized what he still had in his family and friends.

His only alternative would be to expose the existence of his kind and potentially cause the loss of thousands of shifters after the panic set in. As much as their human kin had progressed, they weren't yet ready to embrace someone so alien to them.

Growling softly, he tried to settle his mind and catch sleep while he could. After almost three months, he was bored out of his mind. The only news he caught was hearing people talk as they walked past his enclosure. He hadn't realized before just how much he depended on radio, TV, and his books to keep him company. Solitary by nature, he didn't have much need for interaction with others, yet he couldn't stand being cut off from the world around him.

Being alone, without distractions, he had done more than his share of thinking and dwelling. It was the dwelling that was starting to get to him - the what ifs and self-doubts as he examined his life. Especially the events that had led to his being captured.

Having decided living without his mate wasn't going to work, he had finally gathered his courage, faced the potential ultimate rejection, and had gone to find Danny.

He wanted to rail against the fates but knew he only had himself to blame. First for falling in love with someone he knew probably wasn't capable of settling down, then for going off alone to lick his wounded heart, and finally for shifting into a jaguar before chasing down his mate. His worst mistake of all though was forgetting everything he had been taught about being aware of his surroundings when in animal form. At the top of the food chain he hadn't worried about being dinner. Unfortunately, he forgot to keep an eye out for humans, until it was too late.

The creak of his cage door startled him and had him rising to his feet before he really thought about it. As a dark form slipped into his enclosure, a soft growl welled within him. The scent wasn't altogether unfamiliar, yet completely unexpected.

"Mike? Damn it, man, what have you gone and done this time?"

Michael stalked towards the dark-clad form, close enough that he could hear the other man's heartbeat. As he stepped into a shaft of moonlight, Michael took in the subtle changes to Danny's features. Three years weren't enough to change him completely, but there was a bit more silver in his dark hair, and a few more laugh lines around his golden-brown eyes. Maybe his tan had lightened some, but spending months traipsing around the jungle provided a good deal of cover from the sun.

His scent had also deepened, although it was still as seductive as before. The mate bond called to him, demanding he shift to his human form and reassert his claim on the man standing before him.

"Let's get you the hell out of here. Come on."

Michael shook his head, unwilling to risk his people. Even at the personal cost to him, made worse now that Danny was back in the picture.

"Look, I went to a lot of effort and broke quite a few laws to find an actual jaguar and get his ass here. We have less than twenty minutes to get him unloaded out of the back of my van, get him into this cage and get out of here before the guard comes around. I managed to black out the cameras and make it look like a tree branch took them out, but that's not going to do us any damn good if the guard finds this cage empty. Now get your stubborn ass moving and let's go."

Thanking whatever deity might be watching, Michael moved into the shadows and shifted into his human form. Catching the bundle of clothing Danny tossed at him, he pulled on a pair of black jeans and a long-sleeved black shirt, as well as a pair of worn tennis shoes.

Before he could think about it, he grabbed the other shifter and kissed him hard on the lips. A soft gasp rushed against his mouth, then Danny's mouth parted and Michael swept his tongue past. The taste was so familiar, for a moment Michael was able to ignore the heartache the other man had caused, and savor the touch of another person.

All too soon Danny broke the kiss. "You sure pick the worst times Mike. Thank me later, after we get your ass out of here free and clear."

As he turned on his heel and stalked off, Michael allowed himself the watch the fluid movements of his former lover as he quickly and efficiently reached the edge of the zoo and climbed over the fence. Following fast on Danny's heels, he reached the van moments behind him, in time to see the jaguar he had brought with him open its eyes and stare at them. Still under the pull of the sedative, they closed sluggishly and his tongue lolled out of his mouth.

"Grab his hind end, and I'll take the part that bites. We need to get moving, we're running out of time."

Working together they managed to get the cat over Danny's shoulder in a fireman's hold, and with their superhuman strength, up and over the fence and into his new home and themselves back out and into the shadows with only moments to spare. In the stillness of the night they could hear the guard's tranquilizer-gun bumping against his leg as he came around the corner, a faint beam of light preceding him.

Thankfully the medicine that had been pumped into the jaguar was wearing off and he was becoming alert, his ears twitching as he caught the guard's scent. With a soft roar, he climbed to his feet.

Startled by the sudden aggression, the guard rushed past. Michael breathed a sigh of relief as he kept going, not noticing the two forms hiding in the shadows.

"What if they notice the differences between us?"

His face in shadows as he turned to look at Michael, Danny's voice was still as velvety soft as he whispered back, "That's part of what took me so long. Trying to find a wild jag with similar markings to yours was a bitch. Hopefully, they're close enough that no one will notice, and if they do, so what? Who is really going to think that someone snuck into the zoo to change out animals? Steal, maybe. But swap?"

Michael nodded. Danny had a point; it didn't make any sense. With luck, no one would ever be the wiser. Moving together, almost as if they had coordinated their movements, they scaled the fence again and rushed to Danny's van. As he rushed around to the passenger side, the reality of the moment hit Michael--he was free. And damn, it felt good.

He settled into the passenger seat of the cargo van and watched Danny's movements as he pulled out onto the road, flowing into traffic as if he hadn't just committed any number of crimes. Michael rested his head against the seat and breathed a sigh of relief. Rubbing his palms on the denim of his jeans, he enjoyed the tactile feel of something other than fur.

Not that he hated his animal form, but after three plus months of being a jaguar, the feel of his human body was a blessing. A warm hand clasped his, and squeezed. Michael treaded his fingers through Danny's, content for the moment to forgive him for ripping his heart out. Right then he was thankful that for whatever reason, Danny had come after him.

Which reminded him.

"How did you know I had been taken, and where I was?"

Danny sighed and pulled his hand away. A faint blush stained his cheeks, and Michael almost laughed. Danny really didn't want to answer him, which meant whatever he had to say would be good.

He cleared his throat twice before he grumbled, "I was there and saw them take you."

Michael's eyes widened. Danny had been there? Why?

"Why didn't you stop them?"

"You weren't the only one in animal form. We're just damn lucky that they didn't spot me, or we'd both be shit out of luck."

"Why were you--"

"Look Mike, as much as I'd love to go over the events of the last few months with you, it really can wait. I haven't slept in seventy-two hours. I've been hauling around an illegal cat, scaled fences multiple times in the last few nights, and I am about done in."

Michael nodded his understanding and closed his eyes. His questions would have to wait.

Tentatively, almost as if of its own volition, Danny's hand sought his out again.

The van pulling to a stop jerked Michael awake. With a flush of embarrassment he glanced at Danny to see how he would react. Here he hadn't slept in days, and Michael was the one napping.

A soft smile curved his former lover's lips, a warm glint in his eyes. Michael felt his body responding to that familiar look. Cursing himself for a fool, he smiled back.

"I managed to book us a room for the night. A contact of mine will meet us here in the morning with your passport and ID. You were shown as leaving the country, but not coming back in, so we had some finagling to do to get you registered as returning."

Yet another debt Michael owed this man. Evidently, it wasn't done racking up yet, since he had no money, no clothing other than the borrowed ones on his back, and nowhere to go until he had his wallet and its contents back. The only thing going for him was that he and Danny still wore the same size, so with luck, he would have fresh clothing in the morning.

Suddenly, more weary than he felt he had a right to be given that he had slept the night before, and most of the day, he followed Danny into the hotel room and stopped in shock. There was only one bed.

Glancing at Danny, he noticed him weaving on his feet with exhaustion. Gone was the twinkle in his eyes. In the florescent lights, he could see how bloodshot the other man's eyes were, the lines of flat out exhaustion on his face.

Unwilling to repay his kindness with complaint, Michael pushed his reservations about sharing a bed with his former lover, the man who still had the ability to make his heart race, or bleed, depending on his mood, and sucked it up. His current situation was nothing compared to what he had faced.

With nonchalance he didn't really feel, he settled into the chair next to the bed and started pulling off his shoes. Unzipping his pants, he stood up and announced, "I'm going to grab a quick shower, unless you'd rather take one first?" As he spoke, he let the jeans fall to the floor and pulled the shirt off. Nudity among his kind wasn't anything to be embarrassed about.

Danny shook his head and flopped onto the bed, still fully clothed. "Go ahead. I imagine you haven't had a good washing in weeks. I managed a shower this morning."

Michael had to admit, as he stepped under the warm shower spray a few minutes later, it did feel good. Tipping his head back into the water, he closed his eyes and let the flow wash over him. A quick frolic in the pool while in jaguar form was nothing compared to the sensual decadence of feeling the water rush over bare skin.

Inhaling deeply, he caught the briefest whiff of Danny's scent and his cock reacted. With a soft growl, he cupped his balls and started stroking his cock, savoring the feel of skin on skin, the delight of arousal and impending orgasm. Leaning back against the wall of the shower he bent his knees and thrust his hips forward, rocking slightly with each stroke of his hand over his erection.

It had been so long since he had been able to enjoy the sensation of flesh stroking his cock, that even though it was his own hand, it felt almost painful it was so pleasurable. Much quicker than he would have liked, he could feel the heady sensation of his balls tightening with orgasm. Gasping softly, he tightened his grip and quickened his stroking, until growling softly he got himself off. Mindful of the other man in the bedroom, he didn't linger too long. Danny still needed his own shower, and as much rest as he could get.

Soaping up quickly, he removed the last traces of his orgasm from his stomach and hands, as well as three months worth of grime from his body. A quick shampoo later, and he was ready to head to bed. After turning off the taps, he grabbed one of the hotel's towels and quickly dried off. Wrapping it around his waist, Michael headed back into the bedroom, announcing "your turn", only to be greeted by a soft snore.

Danny was sprawled out on the bed, seemingly dead to the world. Knowing how his ex got when he was completely wiped out, Michael bit back a grin as he started undressing Danny. Somewhere during getting his ex's pants off and getting him under the covers, the towel fluttered to the floor. Michael kicked it aside and went rummaging for a pair of boxers. Thankfully, Danny had thought to bring along a suitcase full of clothing.

After pulling on the silk under-shorts, Michael grabbed the towel and worked it over his hair, removing most of the moisture, before he tossed it back in the bathroom and moved around the room turning out lights, double checking the lock on the door, and then faced the fact that he had to climb into bed with Danny.

The last time they had shared a bed together had been one of his fondest and most bittersweet memories. They had spent all afternoon in bed, teasing and screwing each other senseless. Then while he was lethargic and worn out, Danny had dropped the bombshell on him. He was leaving the country the following week to do research in the rainforest.

Michael would have waited, or worked to free himself up to go with Danny, had the other man asked. It never happened.

Shell-shocked at the idea Danny meant to just walk away after everything they had shared, he had lashed out, which only provoked Danny's temper, and before he knew it, Michael was shouting at the only man he had ever loved to get the hell out and stay gone.

And now he owed him a debt of gratitude he didn't think he would ever be able to pay back.

Sitting on the side of the bed as softly as he could, Michael swung his legs up and under the cover and shifted down. Reaching out, he flipped off the light on the bedside table, and tried to settle himself comfortably. Rolling onto his side, he turned his back towards Danny and closed his eyes.

He wasn't certain how long it took, but he finally started to doze when Danny shifted, rolled onto his side and curled against his back. The warmth of his ex's body was so familiar and so comforting; he snuggled back against him before it registered what he was doing. By then, Danny's hand had cupped his hip, and he had nuzzled his face against Michael's neck.

Trying to pull away, Michael stilled as Danny's hand tightened, and he murmured, "Mike," in his sleepy voice as he cuddled closer. Tears sprung to his eyes at the familiarity of the position. At the moment, he had two choices – wake up a man who had risked a lot to free him, or answer his body's demand that he stay right where he was, and let Danny sleep.

The jaguar crouched inside of him chose that moment to roar it's opinion, and with a soft sigh, Michael relaxed his muscles and let himself sink into Danny's warmth.

Michael woke to the soft glide of a hand running up and down his side, stroking over his hip to brush against his half-erect cock, and back up his body, all the way to his neck. Enjoying Danny's special brand of waking up, he snuggled against the erection pressing between the cheeks of his ass, and let his body awaken.

"Damn I missed you," Danny whispered before pressing soft kisses along Michael's neck.

His words woke Michael completely, just as if he had doused him with cold water. Jerking away, he rolled out of bed and faced the sleepy jaguar shifter. "Missed me? You're the one who walked away!"

Danny flopped back against the bed with a groan, his hair deliciously rumpled from sleep, faint lines from the sheets crisscrossing his body and cheek. "Michael, I don't want to fight."

"Neither do I." With the last word on the subject, Michael stalked off, heading into the bathroom. He was leaning back against the wall, trying to get his emotions under control when Danny followed him into the room.

"But for the record, I didn't walk out on you, you pushed me away."

"The hell I did!" His hands curled into fists at his side as the beast within him sat up and took notice, growling out its pain, the torment the loss of its mate has caused.

"You told me, and I quote 'walk the fuck out the door then, and don't look back.' Sound familiar?"

"I only said that because you had just informed me that you were leaving for a job, and one, didn't know when you would be back, and two, didn't bother to invite me along."

"Jesus, Mike! You'd just started your own career, how the hell could I ask you to be the fifties devoted wife and pack it all up, giving up everything you had worked for, to follow me so that my career could take off. I never intended to leave you!"

Unashamed of the tears clouding his eyes, Michael looked into Danny's sincere golden gaze, noting for the first time the shadows that darkened his eyes.

"Then …"

"Military men have been leaving for months and years at a time, but their families are still there when they get back. I kind of figured given the depth of our love, the bond between us that is stronger than normal love, that we could survive a separation too."

Michael closed the toilet lid and sat down, his shoulders hunched over as the reality settled in. Rather than ask, he had jumped to conclusions.

Danny squatted in front of him. Firm fingers cupped his chin, and lifted his face up. Michael blinked at his tears as Danny leaned forward and kissed him, pressing a soft kiss against his lips. Wrapping his arms around the other man's neck he leaned closer, conscious for the first time that both of them were wearing only boxers. He could feel Danny's chest brushing against his, the curling mat of chest hair tickling his smooth chest.

"Danny," Michael whispered, uncertain just what his ex was expecting.

Danny leaned back and stood. Holding out his hands, he waited until Michael offered his, then pulled him up and into his arms. "I heard that you had left town, and I followed you. I had finished my research, and I was already on my way back to you. You left about sixteen hours before I got into town. That's why I was there when you were taken. I was tired of waiting for you to come to me, and I decided to come back to you."

Michael laughed softly, unable to believe the irony. While Danny was on a plane heading back to the states, he was working his way down to the jungle to find Danny, determined to make him see that they had something worth trying to recapture, hoping that his mate hadn't moved on.

"I can't believe it, the last three months sitting in that cage, and if I had just waiting another day on you, we would have been together."

Danny leaned his forehead against Michael's with a sign, his own chuckle sounding in the small room. "Damn we are a pair, aren't we Mike? Both of us stubborn as hell."

"Yeah."

Despite the heartache of the last few years, the time apart melted away. The bond between mates, true mates, was undeniable, and both he and Danny had acknowledged their meaning to each other years before. Only miscommunication had caused a rift between them, something Michael was determined wouldn't happen again.

His jaguar growled within him, his body humming with long suppressed needs. The idea of stepping out on his mate was as foreign to him as the thought of being without the jaguar, so it had been a long three years, with only his own hand to satisfy his cravings.

Now that his mate was near, and they were both rested, his body was demanding he fulfill its needs. His jaguar was seconding the motion, as with a roar it pushed his body forward, until his cock was pressed tightly against Danny, their bodies lined up together from knee to collarbone.

With a groan of his own, Danny thrust his hands in Michael's hair and pulled him closer, even as his lips sought out his lover's mouth. Tongues dueling, they walked together back into the bedroom, where they fell onto the bed, each needing to assert their claim on the other. Rolling to rest on top of Danny, Michael rocked against his mate, sliding their cocks against each other, the thin layers of silk enhancing the sensation.

His hands turned into paws, sharp claws ripping at the bed sheets as he fisted the material. Shifting so that he straddled Danny, even as he regained control of his body, Michael looked down at his lover, delighting in the darkening of his eyes, the elongation of his pupils, until he was more cat than man.

Faint marking enhanced his natural beauty, until his skin wasn't human, but rather a hybrid of man and beast.

With a growl more savage than a human throat could make, Danny ripped the boxers off of each of them and rolled them over so that Michael was resting on his stomach, with Danny settled between this thighs, his cock pressed against the cleft of his ass.

"It's been a damn long three years Mike. You have a lot of making up to do." In response Michael arched his hips, offering his ass to his lover, needing to feel the velvet heat of flesh sliding into flesh before his nerves exploded.

Sometimes, they had managed to take things slow, to seduce and entice. As he felt the nudging of Danny's cock against his tight ass-ring, Michael knew this wasn't going to be one of those times. Instead it was going to be hard and fast and rough. Just the way his body craved after such a long separation.

As Danny thrust forward, driving deep into his ass, he howled softly at the pain, even as his jaguar trembled in anticipation of being mastered. The beast craved Danny's domination, and Michael's submission. Taking a deep breath, he willed his muscles to relax, and allowed Danny to sink deeper. Which was the sign the other man was waiting for. Moving back, he redistributed his weight and pounced forward, his cock rubbing deliciously against Michael's prostate, even as he forced his body to open wider to accommodate him.

With each thrust his cock grew larger, slowly reaching its full erection as he claimed what was his--the right to his mate's body. Reaching between himself and bed, Michael stroked his hand up and down his cock, coating it with the pre-come steadily leaking from the slit. Fisting it tightly, he worked his hand up and down in time with the thrusts invading his ass.

Growling his need, Michael rocked back into each thrust, his ass clenching around his lover's erection. Danny leaned down and bit his neck, just hard enough to sting. Michael couldn't control his reaction. With a gasp of complete euphoria, he climaxed, his come spurting from his cock onto the sheets beneath him. Danny's balls slapped against his ass as he picked up his pace in response to the involuntary clenching of Michael's ass around his cock.

Grunts and growls filled the room as he pounded away, almost savagely reclaiming his right to Michael's body, his scent marking him as surely as his tight grip and love bites were.

His orgasm sent warmth shooting into Michael's ass. As Danny's cock softened, the evidence of his passion mingled with Michael's on the bed sheets and each man inhaled deeply as they collapsed onto the mattress, their bodies still partially joined.

Danny rolled them onto their sides and curled up tight against Michael, his cock still barely within his lover's ass. Michael clenched his ring tight, needing to prolong the intimate touch as long as possible, after being bereft for so long.

He could feel the steady beat of Danny's heart against his back, the soft slide from fur to flesh as the other man struggled to control his jaguar. Unlike his lover, he hadn't spent three months in animal form, and his beast would be scratching and clawing to get at its mate.

A sensation Michael was very familiar with, having struggled with his own jaguar after some of their more vigorous lovemaking.

"There's still a lot we need to talk about," Danny whispered against his back as he placed small love kisses. Murmuring his consent, but not wanting to dwell on it at the moment, Michael rolled over and slid a leg between his lover's, their bodies shifting and contorting around each others to provide every inch of contact possible.

"I know, but not today. Today, all I want to do is make love to you, maybe shower a time or two, and watch some TV. I've missed out on three months of shows."

Danny pressed a quick kiss against his lips, then moved back enough that they could look into each other's eyes. "Mmmm, tell me about it. There was another cast change on Law & Order." As Michael moaned at having missed such an event, Danny continued on, tormenting him with tidbits about his favorite shows, even as he slowly gentled him, his touch light and infinitely seductive.

A thought occurred to Michael as he was running his hands over his lover's arms.

"How did my blood-work not raise flags? They certainly drew enough of it from me."

Danny smiled that patient smile of his as he waited for the answer to come to him. Thinking it through, Michael tossed out the only solution that made any sense. "Someone in the zoo is a shifter?"

"Yep. Several, actually. Evidently after you were captured and brought in, they saw the abnormalities in the first work-up, and kept you at a zoo where shifters worked. There was no way I could have gotten you out alone, but it couldn't be anything overt. One man had to go in so that if he got caught, it could be blamed as an act of vandalism, leaving it open for others to try again."

Michael digested the information, wishing someone had bothered to tell him what was going on, even as he knew it would have made things worse, waiting, hoping, counting the days as they rolled by.

"So why you?"

"Simple really. I had nothing to lose. With you in here, either I was going to be with you, or whatever happened to me didn't matter. The risk was worth getting you out. Plus …"

His voice trailed off as he reached between them and cupped Michael's cock, his fingers slowly tracing over the vein, causing Michael's eyes to almost cross. "This way, I get to play hero."

His lips curving into a knowing grin, Michael set about giving his mate the reward he was angling for.

MICHELLE HOUSTON

CAGING THE TIGER

ANIMAL ATTRACTION

CAGING THE TIGER

Kyle ran his fingers over the crinkled edge of the letter that he had read so many times he knew the contents by heart. In high school, his teacher had encouraged all of the class to reach out to someone in the community, someone in a field they admired or who they shared a common interest with.

He had chosen a young magician named Meric. At the time, he couldn't really explain what had caused him to write to the illusionist. Certainly it wasn't any great belief in magic. Having grown up in a series of foster homes, many of them not the best environment for a young man, he had long since lost his innocent belief in such things.

Yet the illusionist drew him.

So he had taken a chance and written him a letter, never expecting to hear back.

Now, almost five years later, he had well over a hundred letters and postcards from Mark, the envelopes bearing postmarks from all over the world. Focusing his attention back on the letter he was holding, Mark's latest to him, he closed his eyes and recited the words aloud, needing to hear them, imagining what the other man's voice sounded like.

Kyle,

I have finally managed to book a show in your town, and would like to invite you to attend. Enclosed is a set of five tickets. Please, feel free to invite some of your friends.

I do hope to finally meet you. It's been such a pleasure the last five years.

Sincerely,

Meric/Mark

Opening his eyes, Kyle rubbed his thumb over the signature, tracing the gracefully flowing lines. So much had changed in the last five years. It had only been a year into his pen-pal relationship with the magician that he discovered a dormant side to himself.

Now, he wondered if there were others like him. Thanks to the press about Meric's new act, he had to wonder if his friend carried the same secret in his heart. Could the other man also turn into a tiger?

"Ladies and gentleman, I want to thank you for attending our show. As I am sure many of you are aware, we have added a new feature, and I hope that you find it as spellbinding as you have the rest of the evening."

Kyle watched as Mark, in his Meric persona, wandered around the metal cage, his assistant standing behind it, grasping the colorfully draped rod as he shoved it through all of the bars, one at a time, showing there was no hidden compartment.

"As you can see, this cage is what it appears to be." When he allowed his assistant to pull the rod out of his hands and to the back of the cage on the last set of bars, the chains attached to the top of the cage started to lift it off of the ground. The magician grabbed hold of the side and rose with the cage until he was dangling about ten feet over the stage.

"For the last feat of the evening, I am going to climb inside of this cage and transform myself into a living tiger." Following his words with actions he swung himself onto the top of the cage where he lifted a small door and gracefully dropped through it, resting inside of the cage which would barely hold a full grown tiger.

Kyle leaned forward in his seat as the assistant used the hook at the end of the rod to pull the curtains closed along the front and sides of the cage. Slowly it started to rotate, and the audience went silent.

Then the curtains fell away revealing a white Bengal tiger in place of the man. The audience went wild, clapping and showing their astonishment as the cage was lowered to the stage and the lovely assistant stepped forward and attached a leash to the collar around the tiger's neck. Carefully she opened the cage and led the tiger past the edge of the curtains and off of the stage.

Moments later the illusionist came bounding back out, chasing his assistance, a collar and leash dangling from his neck. When he reached the middle of the stage he stopped and suddenly turned to the audience with a flourish and bowed amid the thunderous applause.

Kyle found himself clapping along almost unconsciously as his gaze trailed over the man who called himself Meric. He wasn't certain, anymore than he had been when he first found out his pen-pal was adding a tiger to his show, but he was coming to suspect that Mark was a shifter, same as he was.

Which he desperately hoped was true, because he had begun to fear he was the only one. His gaze lifted to look the magician in the face and found a pair of piercing blue eyes staring back at him. A cocky half-smile curved his friend's lips, and Kyle knew he had been looking for him.

Almost twenty minutes later Kyle was still sitting in the fourth row from the stage, alone now that everyone else had left. He wasn't certain what he was waiting for. By all reasoning he should be trying to find a way to talk to the illusionist, but hadn't thought of a good way to get past his security. He could only hope that Mark would come to him, since after all, he had invited him.

It was with a start that he realized that he wasn't alone. A black clad form dropped into the seat next to him, the fragrance of sweat, masculine heat, and subtle cologne teasing his nose. Glancing up, his eyes again met startling blue ones. Looking into the eerily light eyes, Kyle fought the bolt of need that was clawing at his insides. Ever since he hit his late teens and the tiger within him made itself known, he had been struggling against the strong urge to mate when an attractive male stirred his interest.

With this male though, it had been almost uncontrollable. So many nights he had closed his eyes and through of the other man, remembering lines in his letters.

Thanks to press photos, he had even had an image to go with the words. All that lacked was a voice. The few recordings of his show he had managed to find were low quality, and you couldn't hear him over the noise of the audience.

Uncertain what he was, he couldn't risk the tiger taking control during the heat of passion and hurting his partner. Forced celibacy was eating at him, but it just wasn't a chance he was willing to take.

And now that he was alone with the object of so many night's fantasies, someone who by all rights probably saw him as just a friend, he could feel his body responding. The tiger was growling softly, demanding to be let out to be petted.

"I see you decided to attend my show. I wondered when I didn't hear back from you, that you might be uncertain about meeting face-to-face." Kyle almost melted at the other man's words. His voice was just as he had imagined it to be, masculine and haunting at the same time; almost musical, with a faint English accent.

"Not uncertain, just, well, uncertain."

"Well now, that was crystal clear." Gracefully Mark shifted in his seat and turned towards Kyle, his long legs stretched out in front of him, his slender hands clasped together on his lap.

Not knowing what to say, Kyle waited to see if Mark would follow his statement with something else. The silence lapsed into uncomfortable, and he found himself squirming under the magician's steady gaze.

"Either way, I'm glad to finally meet the man behind the words."

"Me too."

Kyle fell silent again, watching the rise and fall of the other man's chest as he struggled to form the question he was desperate to ask, even as he feared the answer. If he was wrong, he would most certainly loose the only real friend he had.

Five years of Mark's letters, five years of trust and pouring his soul out to someone and hearing the good and bad in response, was a lot to risk. He knew that. But his tiger was very close to the surface, the roaring louder with each breath he took. He was becoming saturated in the magician's scent, each breath filling his lungs and tormenting him.

His cock was as hard as it had ever been, straining at the seam of his pants, and he had a good idea Mark had to know it.

They had talked about everything, including their shared liking of other men, everything except one key fact--Kyle could turn into a tiger.

Taking a deep breath, he look into Mark's blue gaze and lost his courage.

"You ok there Kyle? You know that you can talk to me. Something is obviously bothering you, has been for a while now judging by your letters. So come on, spill it."

"You know that I'm an orphan," Kyle said the first thing that came to his mind to explain his presence. Mark leaned back in his seat and cocked his head to the side, his eyes taking on a quizzical glint.

"I'm oddly curious to see how this conversation is going to evolve. Go on."

Kyle fidgeted in his seat, not wanting to reveal too much in case he was wrong, but needing to know desperately if he was right about the other man, if he was a shifter.

"I've watched parts of your act on YouTube, and I managed to spot the trick behind the illusion. In all of your acts I could see how you did it, either a slight of hand here, a mis-direction there. Incredible smoke and mirrors really, but not anything beyond a well honed and breathtakingly incredible talent. But that last act, the magic of it all, I had to know. I still have to know."

Mark's firm lips curled into a half-smile, and Kyle felt his pulse jump. Judging by the flaring of the other man's nostrils and the briefest of glances at his lap, Mark knew he was attracted to him. Not exactly where he wanted this evening to go; except his body was screaming yes, this is exactly what it wanted.

"How does this tie in to your being an orphan exactly?"

Although he had told his pen-pal damn near everything about himself, Kyle had never even hinted at what he could do. Now was the point of turning back, if he was going to. After the hell he had been through growing up, trusting someone was enough to make his heart race. Trusting someone with this kind of a secret was torture, but he had learned to listen to his tiger over the last few years, and it was now demanding that he tell the other man about its existence.

It wanted Mark, it wanted to claim him, to be claimed by him. To mate and fuck and make love, and have sex until both man and animal were exhausted. Then to sleep, and upon waking, do it all over again.

Feeling like he was following Alice down the rabbit hole, straight to a trip to the loony bin, he asked straight out, "Is it just an unbelievably good illusion, or do you actually shift into a tiger? Cause I can, and I don't know if I am a genetic freak, or if there are more like me."

The smile on Mark's lips widened, and softened. His blue eyes never broke from meeting Kyle's gaze. Relaxed by it, Kyle didn't expect the other man to move as quickly as he did. One moment he was sitting almost motionless next to him, the next he had leaned down and buried his nose in the valley between Kyle neck and shoulder. After inhaling deeply, he started chuckling.

"Well I'll be damned. I had hoped, but--" Abruptly he cut himself off and sat back hard against the chair.

As he moved, Kyle saw a change come of the other man. He could almost see the energy sweeping over Mark's skin, the barely leashed animal thrusting at his flesh, demanding to be let out to play. Faint strips rippled across the smooth expanse of his arm, then faded away. He was no longer perfectly motionless, despite sitting still. Deep inside of himself, Kyle heard his own tiger's answering roar.

"So you don't think I'm nuts?" Kyle had to be certain. Life had taught him that. Even though Kyle was his friend, things could still go very wrong very quickly.

The magician knew where he lived, knew where he worked and even his daily routine. He could wreck everything if he chose to. Almost worse that the potential fallout was that he could be imagining what he wanted to see, what he craved.

In answer the other man stood and moved into the aisle. From one moment to the next he was gone, and in his place stood a tiger, its black stripes stark against the pearly whiteness of his coat. It gave a faint roar and swiped at him with a paw, stroking it down his leg.

Kyle blinked again and Mark stood before him once more.

"I know you have trouble trusting people Kyle, but I had hoped over the years that you had at least learned to trust me."

Kyle nodded, still shell-shocked by what he had seen. It was one thing to think it, quite another to have seen, and felt, proof.

"I do trust you Mark, probably more than you can understand. I did tell you after all."

"Yes. Yes you did at that." When Mark held out his hand, Kyle unconsciously clasped it and allowed himself to be pulled out of his seat.

"I see that we have a lot to talk about."

Kyle nodded at the other man's words. He had so many questions, he didn't even know where to begin. Unfortunately, the heat of the other man's touch was making it extremely hard for him to think about anything but the fact they were both gay, both shifters, and that he was halfway in love with the other man, and had been for a few years now.

It wasn't anything he was going to burden Mark with though. Some things needed to remain unsaid between friends.

Less than a half hour later he was sitting across from the most charismatic man he had ever met, and possible the answer to all of his questions, in the tight enclosure of a RV. He could hear the sounds of the world around them moving past the metal walls, but in that moment all that mattered was Mark.

If he thought about it, the last five years, all that had mattered to him was Mark. The weekly letters and the postcards from every place he visited.

The magician had shed his cape but kept the tight fitting leather pants and the flowing white shirt, which was molded to his chest. Every breath he took, every shift of his body, drew Kyle's attention. He was hyper-aware of the attraction flowing between them, which they were both working to ignore.

"So where do you want to start?"

Kyle shrugged, uncertain what he wanted to know most.

"Ok, well since it's been a long night, how about I talk, and if you have any questions you just jump in."

Kyle nodded and leaned back against the oversized couch. Mark paused to pull out a tea pitcher from the mini fridge and pour them both a glass. He too a quick sip of his tea, and Kyle watched the muscles in his throat as he swallowed.

"You're not alone. Let me first get that across. I guess growing up without parents you wouldn't know that, but there are probably a few thousand of us worldwide. Tiger shifters that is. There are also others; bear, wolf, leopard, owl, jaguar, hawk, the list goes on. Typically the shifters with the larger populations are predators, since they stand the greatest chance of survival if they embrace their animal and go wild part of the time."

He knew he should be focusing on what Mark was saying, and he was working to process in the information, but at the same time he could feel the weight that had rested on his shoulders easing. He wasn't alone, there were others of his kind. His best friend was a shifter. The man he loved, he could share himself with.

Mentally derailing that train of though, he forced himself to focus on what Mark was saying and not his own hammering need to feel the other man's touch, to feel close to him on a whole different level. To fully open himself up and offer his unconditional trust.

Mark must have seen his eyes glaze over or something because he paused and asked "Kyle, you still with me?"

"Yeah. Um--what about, um, sex." Uncertain how to word what he wanted to know, Kyle blushed and stammered until Mark arched an eyebrow and a half smile curled his lips.

"Are we dangerous when we have sex? Does the cat come out to play? Do we mate for life? What exactly are you wanting to know?"

"Anything, everything."

"Well, that's helpful."

Kyle nodded, and held his breath, anxious to hear the answer but not wanting to get his hopes up.

"Ok, I know that you're gay, since you shared that much. Since you know that I am as well, obviously there are gay shifters. We are in the far minority of course, since nature requires a male and a female to replicate itself. It does differ from beast to beast though. Some shifters clans don't have any, unless they were gay humans who were turned, like the wolves. The wolves incidentally, are one of the few who can add to their numbers by turning humans. Others are more polygamous, and will form multiple relationships at once, often with both sexes. You see that a lot in the bears."

Mark paused and took a drink of his soda before leaning forward, the top of his shirt gaping open, allowing Kyle a view of his chest.

"We can have sex with humans, but we have to control our more animal traits. It's an incredibly rough balancing act though, trying to have a relationship with a human. The need tends to either be to dominate, or to submit. There isn't much middle ground."

Mark leaned forward and covered Kyle's hands with his, and pulled him to the edge of his seat. Their faces only inches apart, he tipped his head and closed the distance until his lips were a breath away from touching Kyle's.

"As for mates, yes, we mate for life. Often we are drawn to our mate, without being aware of it at the time. Then, from one moment to the next, awareness dawns and we just know, down to the very fiber of our being, that the person we are with is the one for us. Now I have a question for you?"

Kyle breathlessly asked "what?" unable to think with Mark so close.

"Are you ready to find out what it's like, the beast riding you as you submit to the need to mate?" Before Kyle could answer Mark pressed his lips against his and swept his tongue past Kyle's parted lips. The feel of the man's mouth on his sent his already strained nerves into overdrive. His cock hardened almost painfully, the blood rushing through it with each accelerated beat of his heart. He almost leapt out of his skin when Mark pulled back.

Kyle swallowed heavily as he tried to figure out how to respond. He wanted Mark, there was no doubt in his lust filled brain about hat, but he wasn't willing to risk their friendship for a roll in the sack.

No matter how good he knew it would feel. His body was on fire, craving Mark's touch. His heart urged him to submit, to allow his body to be claimed. Ignoring the fragile emotions was the hardest thing he had ever done, but he forced himself to pull back.

"God Mark, I wish I could."

The heat of desire in his blue eyes was banked from one moment to the next, and Kyle watched as he sat back, his body tense. Puzzled by the sudden change, he reached out to the other man, needing to comfort him.

As his fingertips brushed against the magician's arm, Mark jerked and muttered an oath.

"If you aren't yet sure of me Kyle, that's fine, but don't fucking tease." His nostrils flared as he exhaled, and his blue eyes darkened. Kyle's tiger stirred inside of him, clawing at his skin, demanding to be let out so he could rub against the other man.

"What? I wasn't. I just needed to touch you. But I don't know, well, what you want from me."

Kyle could hear the hurt in his own voice and wanted to cringe as Mark nailed him with a piercing gaze. He could see the other man working through the last few moments, calculating exactly what it meant. He had seen the same look of intense concentration when he was on stage, right before he performed an intricate movement.

"OK, backing up the miscommunication bus here."

Kyle couldn't hold back the bark of laughter at Mark's comment. His friend certainly had a way with words, something he had greatly come to adore over the years.

"I kissed you, asked you if you wanted to mate with me, and you rejected me. I figure, you don't fully trust me yet, and that it's too soon for you to commit to me. I understand that, knowing what I know. I backed off, knowing I needed to be patient, to wait a while more. But then you reach out, your eyes all soft, your body broadcasting pretty strongly your attraction to me. Your tiger was right at the surface, showing in your eyes. So where are we crossing wires here?"

"Commit to you?" Kyle's heart starting racing as the conversation they had just had played through his mind. Mark had mentioned a knowing when you had found your mate, then he had kissed him, and asked if he was ready to have sex. Now he was talking commitment, and Kyle found himself hoping it meant what he thought, but terrified he was wrong. Curling his fingers into his palm, he winced slightly as his claws started to come out, his tiger as anxious as he was about what Mark would say.

"Yeah, commit. As in give yourself to me, let my tiger claim yours as mate. I get it if you're not ready, but I have to be honest here Kyle, I don't know if I can take hearing about your oat sowing if you need a bit more playing in the field first."

"Are you saying you believe we're mates?"

"Don't you?"

Kyle shook his head, nodded, then shook his head again. He was so confused he didn't know what he knew anymore. Except that his tiger was aware and roaring now, and his cock was hard to the point of spontaneous combustion if he moved wrong.

"Ah, I see now." Without clarifying his statement, Mark stood and held out his hand. Trusting the other man, Kyle reached out and clasped his hand. The magician's palm was warm against his, his fingers long and slender, his fingertips curiously rough and calloused. With strength that was beyond what would be expected for his slender frame he pulled Kyle up and against him. Off balance Kyle literally fell into his arms.

He half expected Mark to push him away, but instead he held him there, his hands slowly moving down to cup Kyle's hips and pull him tighter against his body. Gently, almost tenderly, Mark kissed him, his lips soft, the kiss delicate. Kyle closed his eyes and breathed in the other man's scent, savoring the musky undertones beneath the cologne he wore.

Desire slammed into him, taking his breath away. He wanted Mark, wanted to feel the other man moving over him, to feel the velvet glide of Mark's cock in his mouth, as he wrapped his lips around him, tasting the passion flowing between them.

As Mark broke the kiss, they both shared a sigh that had Kyle's eyes flaring open. Staring into light blue eyes, he fancied he could see his future.

"You are my mate Kyle, and when you're ready, we'll take things the next step. Until then, I will remain your friend."

"What about love?" The moment he said it, Kyle knew how naïve he sounded, even as he realized that somewhere deep inside, somewhere that the hollow existence he had had to date couldn't touch, he wanted to be loved. Craved it.

"Don't you already know that I love you? Hell, I've been halfway in love with you for the last couple of years. I just had to wait until you had time to find yourself. Twenty-two isn't so old in today's world, and I didn't want to rush you. But I've loved you since you opened up to me about your childhood. You trusted me, and I realized then how I felt about you. I just couldn't act on it, because I worried about hurting you, about rushing you emotionally and physically."

Kyle remembered exactly when he had written that letter. He had been halfway through college, thanks to Mark's generous donation and a lot of scholarships and grants, and had found himself feeling lost, alone and completely overwhelmed.

He had reacted out to Mark, writing several letters a day, until at the end of the week he mailed them all out.

Mark's response had floored him. Instead of the "there, there" letter he had expected, his pen-pal had responded in kind, telling him about the loneliness of traveling with a couple so deeply in love that they glowed with it. About the sleepless night in strange hotel rooms, eating more take-out than home-cooked meals in a year.

About the yearning to wake up to someone, to have them cuddle close and just watch the snow fall, or listening to the sound of the rain pounding on he roof.

That's when Kyle realized how deeply he cared about the magician. How much he wanted to be the one laying in the protection of his arms, held close and safe.

Now, standing in the circle of Mark's arms, he did feel safe, and cherished, and desired. His tiger was roaring softly now, content that it was going to get its way, but Kyle wasn't so sure. He wanted Mark with an intensity that made his tremble, but he didn't know if he was ready for a lifetime commitment.

He'd finally made it through college just a few months before, and had found himself wondering what the hell he was going to do with the rest of his life. A degree in graphic design had seemed like a logical choice at the time.

Now, Mark was offering him options he had never thought existed before, and he wasn't sure if he should decide too suddenly. His body however, was making rational thought almost impossible. His heart raced, his cock ached, and his fingertips tingled with the need to trace down Mark's body, to follow the line of chest hair down and see how far it led.

"Fuck all, I waited until you were older, not wanting to rush you. To give you time to find yourself. Yet the first time we meet face to face, here I am doing what I swore I wouldn't. Our tigers are possessive beasts, and it can be a struggle to hold them back, but I swore to myself I wouldn't rush you, that I wouldn't give in my tiger's demand to claim our mate, and here I am doing exactly that."

Kyle listened to the emotion behind his friend, his mate's words, and heard an echo of the loneliness and longing that resided inside of him. He also heard the affection and love Mark felt for him, and his willingness to wait and give him time. Pressing an open-mouthed kiss against the hollow of Mark's neck, he decided to take a chance for once in his life and really trust someone. Experience had taught him not to give lightly, but after five years, if he couldn't trust his best friend, his mate, with his heart, then he couldn't trust anyone.

"Make love to me," he whispered against the side of Mark's neck as he placed soft kisses, his tongue swiping at the salty tang left behind by his sweat. Rather that break their embrace, Kyle felt Mark slowly coax him backwards, guiding him into the bedroom, even as his hands kneaded his ass.

"You have to understand, there's no going back once we mate Kyle. Neither of our tigers will let us walk away. The separation would kill them. We do this, and you're packing up and going on the road with me tomorrow. If you need more time, somehow we will make it work."

Kyle moved his head back and met Mark's earnest blue gaze. The other man really was willing to wait for him to be ready.

"Nothing holding me here." It was all too true. His job he could easily quit, and he doubted it would matter if he didn't give notice, he hadn't been there long enough to be depended on.

As for his apartment, the lease was up soon, and his few personal belongings could fit into two duffle bags. Five minutes and he could be packed and ready to go. Not much to show for twenty-two years of living but given what he had discovered awaited him, what had come before didn't matter so much.

Clasping Mark's hand in his, he turned and led the way to the back of the RV, figuring it was small enough he could find the bedroom. One his first try, he managed to locate it and together they stepped into the room, Mark kicking the door shut behind them.

Suddenly shy, Kyle found he wasn't quite certain just what to do. He wanted to tear his clothes off, climb onto the bed and offer himself up, no preparation, no foreplay. As he moved to do just that, his lover gently clasped his arms and held him still.

Soothingly, he stroked his hands up and down Kyle's arms, raising millions of tiny bumps as the hairs responded to his touch. A soft kiss followed, the glide of Mark's tongue into his mouth melting him at the knees, until he collapsed backwards onto the bed.

Completely uncoordinated in their hurry to disrobe each other, they still somehow managed to get their clothes off, and press their bodies as close together as they could.

Kyle wanted to slow down, for their first time to be what Mark needed, but his body was on fire, his ass clenching with the need for it to be possessed. His cock rubbed against his lover's, leaving tiny drops of come along both their stomachs as the ground against each other.

He could feel his tiger just under his skin, delighting in the scent of his mate. The beast wanted to roll around in the sheets, to soak the scent of Mark's tiger into its skin, to take over their body so that Mark could stroke fingers through its fur. But for the moment, the beast was content to wait, to allow their human forms to cement the bond that would claim their mate.

With a gasp Mark broke the kiss and somehow got the leverage needed to flip Kyle over. Stunned with the almost savagery motion, Kyle rolled his hips back against Mark's groin, thrilling at the feel of a cock rubbing against his ass.

"I've wanted you for so long," Mark whispered as he nipped at Kyle's back, his teeth stinging the sensitive skin with each bite. Deep inside him, Kyle's tiger roared its approval as it coaxed him into a kneeling position, his ass offered to their mate. It was demanding they join, that their mate's scent cover them.

Rather than mount him, as they both were eagerly wanting, Mark moved down until he could nip at Kyle's ass. He jerked at the sting, then rocked backwards as a tongue lapping followed. On and on it went, first a bite, then a kiss or gentle rasp of a tongue, until his back, ass and legs were completely sensitive to the slightest touch. Through it all, his cock and balls hung heavy, eager for their turn. Breathless, he waited in anticipation until with a soft brush of air heralding what was coming, his balls were bite.

Growling at the sensation, Kyle couldn't resist the tiger's urge to come to the surface. He could see his skin striping as Mark lapped at his heavy ball sac, soothing where the sting was, then he bite again. Kyle wanted to be fucked, now! But he couldn't make demands. He had discovered that in the dance between them, he had no choice but to submit to his mate.

Even his tiger, as agitated and needy as it was, still held back -- letting the other man lead their mating.

Warm fingers pressed against his anus, slowly pushing inside while Kyle licked and sucked at his inner thighs and buttocks. A faint click sounded in the stillness of the room, and then a small piece of plastic joined Mark's fingers moments before a small gush of gel flowed into his channel. Mark pulled his fingers back out, and then thrust them in a little deep. Over and over, he worked two fingers in and out of Kyle's virgin hole. He slowly twisted and spread his fingers apart with each retreat and thrust, until finally he worked a third finger in.

Slowly Mark made his way back up Kyle's body, nipping and soothing, as he continued the teasing light and soft thrusts of his fingers.

It was sensual torture, feeling the wet trail Mark's cock left against his heated skin as he worked his way back up until his cock finally pressed against the left cheek of Kyle's ass. As Mark pulled his fingers feel, Kyle let out a soft growl of need, his tiger tired of the soft exploration. It was demanding their join, that they complete the mating. Trembling with need, almost beyond coherent thought, Kyle opened himself at the slightest nudge against his anal ring, and was rewarded by the velvet glide of a cock into his ass.

Mark wasn't done with his sensual torment. As he thrust hard and deep, he sank his teeth into Kyle's neck, drawing out a deep growl of satisfaction as the tiger completely submitted. Kyle arched into the flash of pain that followed his virgin opening giving way to his mate's cock. The sensation of being filled was almost overwhelming. In that moment, he understood what Mark had tried to explain. He could feel Mark's tiger moving restless under his skin, rubbing up against his own beast.

Soft growls filled the room, and Kyle could feel the occasional brush of fur against his back as Mark's tiger fought for control.

Widening his legs, Kyle slid further down against the bed, his cock barely brushing the silken sheet as his lover pounded into his body, the pace picking up with each stroke. His back and legs were sensitive to each motion of his lover, each brush of hair, the slightest touch of skin. He wanted to howl in frustration as Mark kept him just on the edge of orgasm, but never quite pushing him over. His owl tiger was so close to the surface he could feel his claws something out, digging into the sheets and ripping them as he fought to hold on in the maelstrom of passion that was whipping through him.

Panting with need, he kept rolling back into Mark's motions, offering himself, allowing his ass to be claimed, but it wasn't enough.

"I need," he gasped, unable to articulate beyond that point. A growl was his answer, then the faint brush of fur over his legs and back as Mark's tiger fought him for dominance of their mate.

"Mine," Mark rasped against his neck, demanding, not asking. Yet Kyle felt compelled to answer, "Yes, I'm yours. Your mate."

Firm lips pressed against the corner of his mouth, and Kyle arched and turned his head, reaching for the kiss, the thrust of a tongue into his mouth, the motions mimicking the more savage impaling he was getting in his ass.

As Mark's cock surged forward, deeper this time, rubbing in all the delicious spots, Kyle tightened his muscles, clenching at his mate's cock. His balls tightened, and he shifted his hips down enough that he could barely glide his cock along the sheet. Mark's firm hand held him still as he increased the pace, the bed protesting their motions as he claimed him.

Breathless, Kyle submitted, his cock jerking with the first spurt of his come. Bracing himself on his hands, he rolled his hips backward and clenched his ass, holding Mark deep within his body as the warm flood of come started, as his own release continued, the heady scent of their mingling essence filling the small room.

Once again, the collapsed together, this time his lover was still locked inside of his, their mouth still fused as their passions crested.

It was some time later, as he was laying in his lover's arms, long after they had discussed their travel plans and what needed to be done in the morning for Kyle to be freed up to join him, that a stray though whispered across Kyle's mind.

"So what do you do about animal control and all?"

Mark's hand paused in stroking up and down his back for just a beat. Flushing slightly at how convoluted his question had been, he tried again. "There have to be rules and all to having an animal in the show. How do you deal with all of that and still be you dealing with it?"

"How can I be both human and tiger at that same time, during inspections?"

"Yeah."

Kyle could feel his blush deepening. He had to have sounded like a complete fool, but given how mind blowing the last few hours had been, he figured he was due. Added to that his general ineptitude with small talk, and it was no wonder he was making a first class fool of himself.

"There is a couple who travel with me, remember, my assistant and her husband, who is a vet; both of them are tiger shifters. When needed, either can fill in as my tiger. We have a really nice bus that goes everywhere with us, all decked out with plants and rocks. A habitat for our *tiger* to stay in during off stage times. It doubles as our play room when we need to let our beasts free for a little while."

Kyle nodded, uncertain what else to say. Silence reigned in the confines of the RV's bedroom until with a soft groan Mark leaned down and kissed him again. As the other man's tongue thrust into his mouth, Kyle had to fight the urge to crawl on top of him. It felt so good, surrendering to his needs and to his mate, that his tiger was almost impossible to keep caged. It was roaring and scratching at the insides of his body, longing to be stroked as Mark was stroking him, his hands running over his shoulders and chest as he dominated the kiss.

As Mark rolled them over, and settled himself between Kyle's thighs, his tiger quieted down, content for the moment to feel everything through him. Soon enough it would demand it's time, and he had a feeling the RV wouldn't be able to stand up to both of them allowing their tigers to mate. But he had faith that Mark would figure something out. After all, he had figured out how to show himself to the public without anyone ever knowing he was a shifter. And he had figured out how to gain Kyle's trust … and his love.

MICHELLE
HOUSTON

HEALING
THE FOX

ANIMAL ATTRACTION

HEALING THE FOX

Scott finished filling out the admittance form for the baby rabbits that had just been brought in, and then filed away the pink copy. Picking up the white and yellow copies, he headed back into the treatment room where one of the volunteers was busy working on the babies, trying to re-hydrate them and patch them up from their run-in with a cat, while at the same time not kill them. Baby rabbits were notorious for simply dying in your hands. Unable to handle the shock, their little bodies just gave out.

Shaking his head at the whole mess, Scott clipped the paperwork onto the board for the treatment room and headed down the hallway to Isolation Room 6, where the mammals were kept. He'd been waiting for just such a moment all day. Normally up to their asses in injured animals this time of year, it had been an unusually light day ever since the fox had been brought in, although that could and probably would change at any moment. The injury to the creature came from a run in with a car. The driver had left the fox lying on the side of the road with its leg broken. If the state trooper hadn't been passing by, and hadn't attended a lecture Scott gave on rehabbing injured wildlife, the fox might not have made it through the night.

Scott gritted his teeth, irritated by having to wait for a moment alone with the injured animal. As much as he loved his job, being a mentor was frustrating when another shifter came in. He couldn't risk anyone finding out his secret, or worse, thinking him insane and firing him.

So, he had to be very careful how he handled certain cases.

As he pulled the door closed behind him, he paused a moment to look out the window to make sure no one else had finished up and was heading his way. Satisfied that he was safe for the moment, he crouched down in front of the cage. The fox stared at him, almost listless from dehydration. Already twice today he had had a tube pushed down into his stomach to get water and nutrients back into his system.

"I know you're probably too out of it to understand me, but I'm going to get you out of here as soon as I can. I leave in a few hours, and since I am set up for rehab at home, I can take you with me. I just need you to hang in there a little bit longer."

Opening the cage door, Scott curled his fingers around the other shifter's head and gently scratched, letting the animal get a good whiff of his scent and testing the man's control over the beast. Shifters were always their most dangerous when injured in animal form. Instinct took center stage, and accidents can and did happen.

The last shifter he had treated was a perfect example. Two days passed before Scott found out about him, and by then the wolf had been too far gone. His human half completely surrendered to its beast after being shot, operated on, then locked in a cage. The wolf had gone insane, and Scott had to contact the nearby council to come and take him.

This time, though, he wasn't about to let that happen. This creature was one of his kind, and he wasn't about to lose the man inside to the fox. "Can do you do that for me? Hang in there?"

In response the fox shivered slightly, tipping his head into the scratching. Scott stayed with him longer than he should have, rubbing his hand over slightly bristly fur, knowing the other shifter needed touch to keep him from feeling isolated and drowning in hopelessness.

"I have to go, fella, but I will be back in just a little while. Remember, hang in there."

With a last scratch, Scott pulled his hand out of the cage and closed the door just in time. Glancing up as a shadow crossed over him, he met the gaze of one of the volunteers. He could hear her voice through the door as she called out, "Scott, I'm all done with the mice cages. Anything else you need me to do?"

Growling softly at the interruption, he spared one last glance at the now sleeping fox and then climbed to his feet to finish out his day.

Almost six hours later, he had completed the paperwork to take the fox home with him. It was frowned upon to take recently admitted animals home so soon, but with the cages quickly filling, the nature center relied on home rehabbers more and more to juggle the overflow. Given that the fox sustained no internal injuries, and simply suffered dehydration, some bumps and bruises, and a broken leg, he was a lower priority for constant care.

Which was actually more of a blessing than normal. Not only was he not too badly injured, but the sooner Scott could get the other shifter to his place and settled in, the better all around. With space, and the comfort of another of his kind, the fox should heal quickly and be able to shift back within a few days.

With Scott being a staff member and a frequent rehabber, there really wasn't a big issue made over his taking the poor guy home with him. It also helped that Scott didn't have to be back in for another four days, thanks to the cutback in funds.

The next few days passed in a blur. Scott fed and cared for the birds in his flight pen and took care of the fox, in addition to his day-off catching up on chores. It never failed to amaze him how much laundry one man could accumulate in just ten days. Although, it probably didn't help that he had work-out clothes, work clothes, and then around the house clothes for every day.

As he was tossing another load of towels in the dryer, he couldn't help but reflect on his newest guest. The injured fox's leg was healing fairly quickly, and he had started to show some signs of spirit by the end of the second day. He even yipped a few times when Scott came into the room and didn't spend several minutes stroking his fur. It was definitely an encouraging sign that he craved the contact. Only time would tell if the human inside would remain trapped, or if he would be able to transform.

Having been there once himself, which had caused him to seek out the opportunity to volunteer at the nature center, he had a fairly good idea of what the other man must be going through. Being trapped in his animal form, unable to allow the animal free reign of the body, had to be complete hell. Injured, possibly frightened, and feeling isolated from anyone and everyone he knew, the man inside the fox had to be going stir crazy.

Only the fact that the fox didn't attack him, and responded to his voice and touch gave Scott any hope of the man's recovery. By now, he should have been up and moving around, testing the limits of his body. Instead he still lay on the bed, almost listless. Scott hoped it was simply boredom, as the man waited on the animal's leg to heal.

Grabbing the freshly laundered sheets, he headed down the hall to change out the bedding on the guest bed. Scott entered his guest room to find a naked man lying on the bed. Curled up on his side, he had his heels tucked against the backs of his thighs, his hands folded between his knees. Piercing, golden eyes followed Scott's movements as he crossed the room with the laundry.

Carefully balancing himself, he knelt down beside the bed and met the shifter's gaze head-on.

"Do you remember how you got here?"

With the slightest of movements, the other man nodded. His red hair fell into his eyes with the motion, and very slowly Scott raised his hand and tucked the errant strands behind his ear. Cautious at first, he grabbed hold of the top sheet and tugged it up and over the other shifter, covering him. Although he rather enjoyed the sight of the man's body, it just seemed wrong to ogle him when he was still obviously out of it.

As near as they had been able to tell, he had been lying on the side of the road for two days, unable to get water, and unable to move out of the heat of the summer sun. Just one more day would have done him in.

"I need to take a look at your right leg. Can you extend it?"

In answer, the other shifter slid his leg out from under the sheet and held it still while Scott examined it to make sure it had healed properly. Thankfully, despite the pain he had to have been in, the other shifter had been smart enough not to attempt to shift back to his human form.

The majority of the books got it wrong in that regard. Shifting did not heal injuries. In fact, the realignment of molecules that occurred in going from one form to another could further the damage since it drained energy that was better used to heal. The best option was to stay in the same form the injury happened in, and to let his heightened metabolism and immune system respond.

"It looks like everything is good. So, you should be back to normal in a few more days." Unless, that was, his mind had taken a hike. "Do you remember your name?"

The shifter licked his lips and paused, seeming to search for the information. "Christian. Chris."

Heaving a mental sigh of relief, Scott continued to ask Chris questions, slowly pulling out the information he remembered from his injury and the past few days. After several minutes, he called a halt to the conversation.

"Alright then, let's get some food into your system."

Christian tried to move himself upright in the bed, but Scott ended up having to help him. As he pressed against the other man's chest, Scott tried to ignore the rush of arousal that swept over him. The man needed his care, not his lust.

Forcing that thought into the forefront of his mind, he headed to the kitchen to cook up a quick can of soup. Returning as soon as he could, he found Chris leaning back against the wall, his dark lashes shadowing his cheeks as he dozed.

Regretfully, Scott shook him awake, knowing he needed food as much as rest at this point in his recovery. As he settled several pillows behind his patient and sat down on the bed beside him, the tray settled over his lap, he watched Chris--the fluid way he moved his hands despite his exhaustion, the way his throat bobbed with each swallow, the way his lips pursed around the spoon.

Working together, they managed to get the warm soup and most of the bread into Chris before he started nodding off. By the time soft snores filled the room, Scott was completely under his spell. Adjusting his erect cock to a more comfortable position, he headed out of the room, leaving the door open a crack where he could hear if his patient needed anything during the night.

As he undressed and stepped into the shower, he couldn't help but remember how Chris had looked, his tan skin against the soft cream of the sheets. His lithe body completely uncovered, the golden highlights in his red hair were a perfect match to his fur in animal form.

Sliding a soap-covered hand down his chest, Scott gave in to the urge and stroked his cock, gliding up and down the length as he fantasized about the other shifter. He wasn't sure enough yet what his personality was to determine if he would be dominate or submissive, but Scott hoped Chris was a switch like him, someone who felt comfortable in either role. Unlike the larger predator species, Scott hadn't had to worry too much about controlling himself with human partners, so he had never lacked for companionship, but there was something about being around another fox shifter, especially one as attractive as Chris, that was giving him ideas about the future.

Judging by the faint hints of pheromones that had teased at his nostrils when he helped the other man to sit up, Chris was attracted to him.

Closing his eyes, he glided his hand up and down his erection, rolling his palm over the tip, then stroking back up. Scott could feel his balls tight against his body, the need to orgasm riding him hard. Pumping his fist faster, he tightened his grip. Up and down, up and down, blood throbbing in his cock, he jerked himself off until with a soft groan he came. Jets of come splattered against the shower wall as his orgasm claimed him, almost sending him to his knees. In his mind's eye he could see the redhead kneeling before him, mouth open, eager to drink his come.

With a soft sigh, he leaned back against the cool shower wall.

The next day passed fairly quickly, with Scott finishing up the last of his chores and spending as much time as he could with his house guest between his frequent naps. Although Chris continued to nod off during their conversations, Scott came to know the other shifter, and liked having him around. They shared a lot of the same views on what Scott considered the important topics, and there was certainly a spark of attraction every time they came into contact with each other.

Scott also found that his reaction to the other man was happening on many different levels. Intellectually he found him stimulating. Physically, there was no doubt about his attraction to the other shifter. It was the deeper, instinctive level that bothered him. His inner animal was responding to the other man, clawing and yelping to get out, to rub its fur along Christian's body, to share scents.

He had had lovers before, and while his fox always found the experiences enjoyable, there had never been a battle for supremacy. With Chris, he found it hard to deny his animal equal time. He also couldn't deny the bond that he felt forming between them, driving by an instinct older than time. He was mating, and if he wasn't careful, he would lose a part of himself when he had to let Chris go.

Early the next morning, after another restless night fantasizing about the other man, Scott headed off to work. Before he left he made sure that Chris had everything well within reach, including a phone. Time passed fairly quickly as he hit the ground running--from the time he walked through the doors, until he finished caring for the last animal almost eleven hours later. In between patching up critters, changing and cleaning cages, and feeding a whole passel of babies, he had managed to grab a light lunch around one. During the course of the day he had taken a few breaks to call his home and check on Christian, assuring himself that the other shifter was indeed okay.

Tired, hungry, and completely drained, Scott pulled into his driveway almost twelve hours after he had left it. The sun was setting, and he barely managed to drag his ass out of his car and up the steps. As he put his key in the lock, he debated which take-out place would be healthiest for the recovering fox.

Upon opening the door, the thought fled his mind. The most delicious scents were coming from his kitchen, scents he hadn't ever smelled in his home. Being a barely passable cook, he had no use for the dozens of spices his sisters insisted he needed to keep on hand, let alone the raw ingredients needed to make full-on meals.

Most meals he consumed at home consisted of take-out or microwavable food.

As he headed down the hall towards the kitchen, the aroma grew stronger, yet it was mixed with a light hint Chris' natural scent. Fairly territorial by nature, his fox yipped at the indignity of someone other than him marking the house, yet it was also aware of the heady scent of male.

Of desirable, unmated male.

Chris himself had confirmed the fact, when he had asked if there was someone that needed to be called. The other man had met his gaze and responded that he wasn't seeing anyone, and hadn't been for a while. Looking into the golden depths, Scott had found himself falling even more under the younger man's spell. He wanted to keep him, to claim him as his mate.

As he reached the doorway, an off-key rendition of *I Can't Dance* greeted his ears. Leaning against the doorway, he watched as Chris moved, the borrowed jeans hanging low on his hips, his bare back undulating as he shimmied around the room in time to Genesis.

Holding up a spatula, he sang into it as he worked his way to the sink, where he dipped it into the waiting water. With smooth motions, he scrubbed the plastic, then rinsed it off before repeating his motions another time. Finally satisfied, he set it into the drainer and spun on his heel.

As he swung around, his gaze landed on Scott.

It was almost comical, the way his eyes widened, the slight curl of his lips, and the blush that stained his skin from his forehead down into his chest. Redheads really couldn't hide embarrassment.

"I was mmmmaking you dinnnnner," Chris stammered out.

"So I see." Scott couldn't help but reflect on how amazing it was. Just moments before, he had been dragging his ass just to get this far, but at the sight of Chris' bare chest--the faint red hairs curling around his nipples and dusting his stomach, blazing a trail down to the waistband of the jeans--and he was wide awake More than, really. If his cock was anything to judge by, he could go all night and into the next day without pause.

"I really appreciate it. I was just debating which delivery place to call for dinner."

"Not while I'm here." If anything, Chris' blush deepened. He really was charming, and the idea of keeping him was incredibly tempting.

Raised with four sisters, Scott couldn't resist teasing, especially given his own discomfort with the topic. "Oh, really now. Staking your claim, are we?" As Chris' face flamed fire engine red, Scott wondered if he had gone too far. Likely the other shifter hadn't been the butt of two older sisters' jokes and the bane of two younger ones. More than likely he also wasn't feeling the irresistible pull of a mating bond.

"I didn't mean … I wasn't trying to …"

Pushing off from the wood frame, Scott moved towards the other shifter and rested his hand lightly on his shoulder. "I know that. Sometimes, my inner devil overrides the better angels, and you see what results." He resisted the urge to stroke his hand up and down Chris' arm.

"Um, good. I wouldn't want you to think that I was… I mean, I don't want to make it seem like … I do find you attractive, but I know that you might not … Oh hell, dinner's almost ready."

Before he could second guess himself, Scott allowed his inner beast to take over. He stepped closer to the other shifter, just enough to brush lightly against him. Tipping his head down, he moved slow enough so the other man had more than enough time to pull away before their lips met. At the heat of contact, Scott slid his hand down from Chris' shoulder along the lines of his arm and cupped his elbow.

Pulling him closer still, he nudged his tongue against the opening of Chris' mouth until he was granted entrance.

A rush of pleasure swept over him, beginning at his lips but swirling down his body until his cock strained against the zipper of his jeans. The smell of desire rapidly filled the room as the two battled for control of the kiss, their mouths mashed together, teeth clicking as their tongues rubbed together, thrusting and parrying.

Breathless and a bit lightheaded, Scott finally broke the kiss and moved back. Looking at the other shifter, he could see Chris was just as affected. His cheeks were flushed, but not with embarrassment. His eyes had a faint glazed look, and his cock strained against the fly of his borrowed jeans.

For a brief moment, Scott wished the jeans were just a bit looser, so that the head of the other man's cock could nudge its way free. As it was, he had to fight the urge to unzip the denim, sink to his knees, and suck him off.

Clearing his throat, he tried to put some distance between them before he said to hell with dinner, lifted Chris onto the dining room table, and feasted on him instead. "Do I have time take a quick shower?"

"Barely."

As he stepped under the warm spray a few minutes later, Scott couldn't help remembering his shower from the night before. If he closed his eyes, he knew he could easily imagine the redhead's hands touching him, stroking the soap over his body. But, with a hot meal on the table, one that was home-cooked and didn't require him to make it, a quick orgasm was going to have to wait.

Although, if he played his cards right, the night might end with one.

Shaking the thought away as soon as he had it, Scott focused on two words. Patient. Houseguest. He kept repeating them in his head as he climbed out of the shower, dressed, and headed back into the kitchen. It didn't matter how much his cock ached to sink into the redhead's ass, or how much his own ass begged to be plundered. Chris was his houseguest, his patient, and he had no clue what the other shifter had planned beyond recovering. He certainly had no right to ask him to stay, nor did he want Chris to out of a sense of obligation. If they mated, it was going to be at Chris' initiative, not his.

While he had been in the shower, Chris finished up dinner and managed to set the table that sat in the corner of the room, a homey little breakfast nook area. Settling himself into his normal seat, he waited while the redhead settled himself across from him before he picked up the salad tongs and dished himself a small portion before handing the bowl over and repeating the process with the spaghetti. Reaching for the warm and golden Italian bread that smelled so fantastic, Scott tore off a small corner and chewed slowly, savoring the flaring of taste on his tongue.

It had been a long time since he enjoyed fresh baked bread. Scott was rather intrigued that Chris managed to put such a meal together from just the stuff in his pantry and freezer. Scott's sisters insisted on keeping his stocked up with options, but most of the space was filled with quick fix meals.

"So, how was work today?" At Chris' innocent question Scott almost choked on his dinner. For a brief moment he allowed himself to imagine how it could be, coming home to the svelte redhead each night. It was an altogether too tempting fantasy.

As soon as he got his coughing under control, his eyes still watering, Scott managed a "fine."

A soft chuckle greeted his response and he looked into Chris' golden eyes to see them twinkling with devilish glee. In response Scott threw the rest of his bread at him, then immediately wished he hadn't. As the other shifter fished the flaky treat out of his lap, Scott snatched it back and took a bite, which earned him another chuckle.

Not that he minded. He could grow used to Chris' soft laugh.

Shaking his head at his fanciful notions, he tried to tame his body's response to the soft sounds. All too easily he could hear what other sounds the slender man would make as Scott pounded his ass. If he closed his eyes, Scott knew not only would he hear the slurping moan of a mouth around his cock, but he would also be able to feel the phantom sensations.

"What about you?" Scott cleared his throat and tried again when his voice came out raspy and hoarse. "How was your day?"

"Lonely, but relaxing. I changed the sheets on my bed and finished up the laundry you had left over. I hope you don't mind." Christian tipped his head slightly as he spoke, sending a cascade of red locks down to his cheeks.

Scott curled his hands into fists on his thighs, resisting the urge to reach out and brush the soft hair back so that he could see the other shifters face. Watching Chris' facial expressions became was becoming almost an obsession with him. "Mind? Hell, I certainly don't. Feel free to do whatever around here, just don't tax yourself. You're supposed to be healing, not housecleaning for me."

Chris nodded and flashed him a quick smile before returning to his dinner. The rest of the meal passed mostly in nonsense talk as they discussed some of the things Scott did with his job and the home rehab. Chris, he found out, was wrapping up his college degree. Temporarily out of school for spring break, he had decided to go camping and let his animal roam for a few days. He was expected back on campus in two days.

As soon as that registered, Scott lost his appetite. Settling back in chair with a sigh, he pushed his plate away and tried not to mourn the loss of something he never truly had. "Where did you leave all of your gear?"

When Christian named the little state park about forty miles away, Scott offered to take him there as soon as he was done with dinner.

"If it's okay with you, I'd actually like to stay tonight and head there tomorrow." As the other shifter stood up and came around to stand behind him, Scott held his breath. A soft kiss pressed against his neck, then the soft glide of a hand ran down his arm. Closing his eyes, he allowed himself a brief moment of fantasy before he had to face the reality that, at best, he could have one night with Chris. One night with someone he could easily picture spending a lifetime with. Because, as soft spoken as the other man was, he possessed a core of steel, evident by the fact he had survived two days alone on the side of the road, dying, and still remained sane. He was a man Scott could easily be proud to call his mate.

Scott could see where Chris would want to have sex, to reaffirm to himself that he was indeed alive. And he'd be a shit to take advantage.

"I uh, have no problem with you staying another night, but you don't have to do anything you don't want to, Chris." It took everything he had to get the words out, and still he felt they weren't enough. Scott almost fell out of his chair as it was suddenly jerked back from the table. Without any warning the lithe form of the other shifter straddled him and dropped into his lap, his warm svelte body sending shivers of awareness and need throughout Scott's body.

"I know. I want this."

Before Scott could caution him again, the other shifter wrapped a hand around the back of his neck and held him still as he plundered his mouth. Moaning at the intimate touch of another man's tongue rubbing against his, Scott gave himself up to the sensations. He had fought his attraction to the other man since day one. His inner fox had scratched at his insides, wanting to get out and curl around the injured shifter, offering the comfort of warmth.

Now that the man was seated on his lap, grinding so deliciously against his erect cock, Scott couldn't hold to what he should do, which was to get up and walk out of the room, leaving temptation behind. He might be a shit for it, but he surrendered to his need and the other's shifter's desire and wrapped his arms around Chris' back and pulled him tighter against his body.

They kissed for what seemed an eternity, each struggling to give and receive the pleasure of two men discovering each other. Their hands roamed as they wished, stroking over arms and chests, along backs and thighs. It was a heady sensation to learn just where to touch the other shifter and to have him discover where Scott liked to be stroked.

The teasing and foreplay slowly drove Scott out of his mind. His cock was so hard he felt like he would burst with need, but he enjoyed Christian's touch too much to move things any further. He was also determined that if they were going to go any further, it would be at the other man's coaxing.

Relaxing into his chair, he rocked his hips slightly, rubbing his denim covered cock against the cleft of Chris' ass, savoring the delicious friction. It didn't help to control his raging needs, but he was too far gone for that. If he didn't come soon he was going to lose his mind.

As suddenly as Chris had sat down, he broke the kiss and stood. His body was surrounded by the light coming through the window from the setting sun, and Scott shuddered at how it wrapped him in red warmth, glistening almost like fur. When Christian's hands went to the waist of his jeans and started pulling his shirt free, Scott's breath held. He watched, savoring the sight of his lover stripping for him, hurriedly removing one of the layers that stood between their naked bodies rubbing together, joining together.

He could handle whatever Chris wanted to do: blowjobs, hand-jobs, getting his ass fucked or doing the ass fucking. It didn't matter. What mattered was the slender yet masculine body that was now standing before him completely nude as Chris unzipped his pants and let them slide to the floor. Chris' cock was hard and flushed with need, the crown blood red and weeping, drops of pre-come glistening on the tip.

Scott licked his lips in anticipation of sucking the other man's cock into his mouth, and tasting the tangy sweetness than would be unique to the other shifter. Carefully he stood, aware that his pulse was racing. He was just about to pull his own shift free when Chris stepped against him, his slender yet firm hands covering Scott's. "Let me," he whispered, and Scott could deny him nothing.

Standing there passively, he allowed the other shifter to slowly peel his shirt over his head. He couldn't hold back a soft moan as Chris tossed his shirt aside and knelt in front of him, carefully helping him out of his shoes and socks before turning his attention his belt. Still kneeling, his face on crotch level, Chris slowly unbuckled the belt and slid it free from the loops while Scott watched, mesmerized. Christian slowly licked his lips, his golden eyes alight with anticipation and desire.

As his pants were unzipped and his cock broke free from restraint, Scott wanted to pull the other man to his feet and pound into him, but he waited in breathless anticipation to see what the other shifter would do. As warm lips parted and wrapped around his erection, Scott's knees buckled. Grabbing onto the table beside him with one hand and his lover's shoulder with the other, he held himself upright while Chris licked and sucked on his cock, learning his taste.

Standing there in his kitchen in broad daylight, getting the blowjob of his life, Scott didn't think he could feel any happier or sadder at the same time. It was going to rip him apart to let the other man go, but he knew he had to. Chris had a life to return to, and he had no claim on him.

Shaking his head at himself, he pushed the thoughts of tomorrow aside and focused on building the memories of today that would sustain him. He could feel his balls tightening, heralding his orgasm. Groaning at the loss, he pushed Chris back, determined that he wasn't going to orgasm in his lover's mouth. There was time enough to that throughout the night. This first time, he wanted to be buried balls deep in the other man's ass.

Almost like he was reading his mind, Chris gracefully got to his feet. Unable to hold back, Scott grasped the other man and pulled him close for a kiss. Desperation laced his motions as he took possession of Chris' mouth, giving no quarter. He was determined to mark the other man, to lay some claim that he would feel even after they parted.

Soft moans and growls filled the room as their inner foxes pushed close to the surface, thrilling in the animalistic mating they had moved into. This was no longer the civilized learning and exploring of two men, it had transformed into the heated battle between two shifters, each vying for domination even as they thrilled in their forced submission. Finally winning the battle of wills, Scott broke the kiss and turned Chris in his arms, pressing him against the table.

Without coaxing, Christian grasped the edge of the table firmly and arched backwards, rubbing the smoothness of his ass against Scott's cock. Leaning his face into the curve of Chris' shoulder, Scott bit down slightly, holding the tender flesh between his teeth as he guided his cock into the waiting, and welcoming, ass of his lover. His cock was well lubricated by saliva and his own pre-come, and glided in easily, pressing forward firmly and hard. Rather than pull away, Chris arched his back, shifting his hips just enough to force Scott's cock all the way in.

Both men were panting with need by with time Scott was balls deep, his cock throbbing. Reaching around Chris' waist, he grabbed the other shifter's cock in one hand while he used the other to hold him steady. Stroking up and down the other shifter's erection, he timed it to his own strokes, driving them both wide with need.

Alternating soft nips and kisses against Chris' neck, shoulder, and back, he claimed the other man, his cock thrusting and withdrawing in an increasing pace until they were both almost mindless with the need to climax. Grinding his hips and pounding deep, Scott continued to work the other man's cock in his hand, holding on somehow until he felt the other shifter's cock jerk. A warm spurt of come landed on the table, followed by another and another as he milked Chris' cock with his hand.

While his lover still trembled with the quakes of his orgasm, his ass muscles fluttering and clenching tight, Scott allowed his head to drop to rest against Chris' shoulder as he pounded harder and faster, his thrusts growing shallower as he embraced the fury of his own orgasm. Growling at the molten sensations flooding from his cock, Scott kept pumping his hips, allowing Chris to milk the last drops of his come from him.

Weak and completely sated, he slipped free from Chris' ass and dropped into his chair. With a small smile curling his lips, Scott watched as his lover slowly pushed himself up from where he was resting, almost boneless, against the table. Chris managed to turn and somehow straddle him again, his now limp cock brushing against Scott's stomach, leaving a faint trail of his come.

Scott wanted to rub it into his skin, forever marking his body with Chris' scent, but restrained the urge. Tonight was all he could have, and he was determined to enjoy it without forcing any kind of a bond between them, no matter how much his fox was biting and clawing for him to do so.

It took some doing, but he managed some time later to stand, with Chris wrapped around him, and carried the other shifter to the bedroom where he proceeded to spend most of the night creating memories. At some point, he even allowed his fox to take control, and shifted form, rubbing his sleek body along Christian's until the other shifter indulged him and shifted, too, provoking a bout of wrestling and playing that ended with them shifting back to their human forms and finishing what their teasing had started.

When the next day dawned bright and clear, Scott woke to the delicious sensations of warmth around his cock. Fluttering his eyes open, he found Chris straddling his body, his back turned towards him, slowly rocking in his lap, teasing his ass-ring with the head of Scott's cock. Without missing a beat, Scott grabbed the phone off the nightstand and called in to work. It was hell trying to keep his voice steady as Chris grasped his cock and guided it to where it wanted to be and started bouncing on him, with the delicious sounds of their flesh slapping together echoing in the still room.

Finishing the call as quickly as he could, Scott disconnected and tossed the phone aside, then spent the majority of the day mating and sleeping with his lover.

He was certain of it, in a way he had always longed for, but now he almost wished he had never experienced this--Christian was his mate, and destined to rip his heart out. Determined that the other shifter never know, Scott poured all of his heartache and passion into claiming his mate's body, silently offering all he had to give.

When evening dawned, he forced himself to remain calm and steady as he helped Christian dress again in borrowed clothes and drove him to his campsite.

"You're always welcome to visit, you know. I have an apartment neat campus."

Scott nodded, unable to vocalize his needs. He wouldn't put Chris in the position of having to chose, no matter what his body was demanding. The mate bond was so strong; he could feel his heart ripping in two with every breath he took.

"I'm going to miss you," he finally settled on, knowing it was only a drop in the bucket of his feelings, yet was a safe statement. "And my home is always open to you. Should you wish to come back ..." Scott's voice trailed off as his throat tightened.

Chris nodded and stepped into his arms, his warmth and affection almost enough to help Scott bring himself back under control. His fox was clawing at his insides, demanding he convince Chris to stay.

With a bittersweet kiss, Scott pulled away and said goodbye. Without looking back, he climbed back into his truck. The other shifter had promised he would come back to visit as he cuddled against Scott's chest, but Scott didn't allow himself to hope that Chris actually would.

It was heading into early June when a volunteer came hurrying into the center, jabbering about someone really needing to see Scott. Heaving a soft sigh, he wearily turned from where he was examining a hawk with a broken wing, gave instructions to the volunteer working with him to finish up, then headed out of the room. Pinching the bridge of his nose, Scott tried to summon an urge to give a shit about whatever it was someone needed to see him about. The last few months he hadn't slept well, and had even less interest in eating.

May had come and gone, the school semester had ended, and still his mate hadn't come back. Despite knowing it happened that way sometimes, that one mate would feel the bond stronger and long before the other, it nonetheless tore him in two thinking about Chris, wondering if he had found someone else.

If he would ever come back.

As he stepped out into the lobby, Scott came to an abrupt stop. Silhouetted against the setting sun stood a familiar form. Blinking rapidly to push away the tears that sprung to his eyes, he tried to force his mind to quit playing tricks on him. The other man may have a similar shape as Chris, but it wasn't him.

As the other man moved towards him, Scott's heart skipped a beat. Soft knuckles brushed against his cheek, whipping away the tear that had broke free.

"Miss me?" As Chris' voice broke, Scott grabbed the other shifter and pulled him close, his lips slamming down over him. Uncaring about what his co-workers thought, he laid claim to his mate's mouth, determined that he show Chris just how much he had missed him.

Hands trembling, he cupped Chris' cheeks and pulled back, staring into his beloved's golden eyes. "Don't leave me again," he whispered, unable to stop himself. He knew that the other shifter had to see in his eyes just how badly he had hurt.

Christian's half smile melted his heart. "I won't. It tore me up to leave you, but I needed to finish my degree. I couldn't walk away from it, not since I was that close. I figured I had time, that I could come back and we could see where things went. I didn't know you had bonded to me, I didn't know until just now."

He wrapped his arms around Scott's waist and pressed his face against his chest. "God, I missed you so much."

At his lover's pain laced words, Scott's arms tightened for a moment, then he forced himself to pull back. Clasping Chris' hand in his, Scott led him into the back room and away from prying eyes. He needed to finish up, but at the same time he couldn't bear to let the other man out of his sight.

It only took him an hour to wrap up the last minute details, far longer than he would have liked but it was unavoidable. He had responsibilities that he couldn't shirk, something that he knew Chris would understand.

Then, finally, they were able to head home where they spent the night, and every night thereafter, in each other's arms.

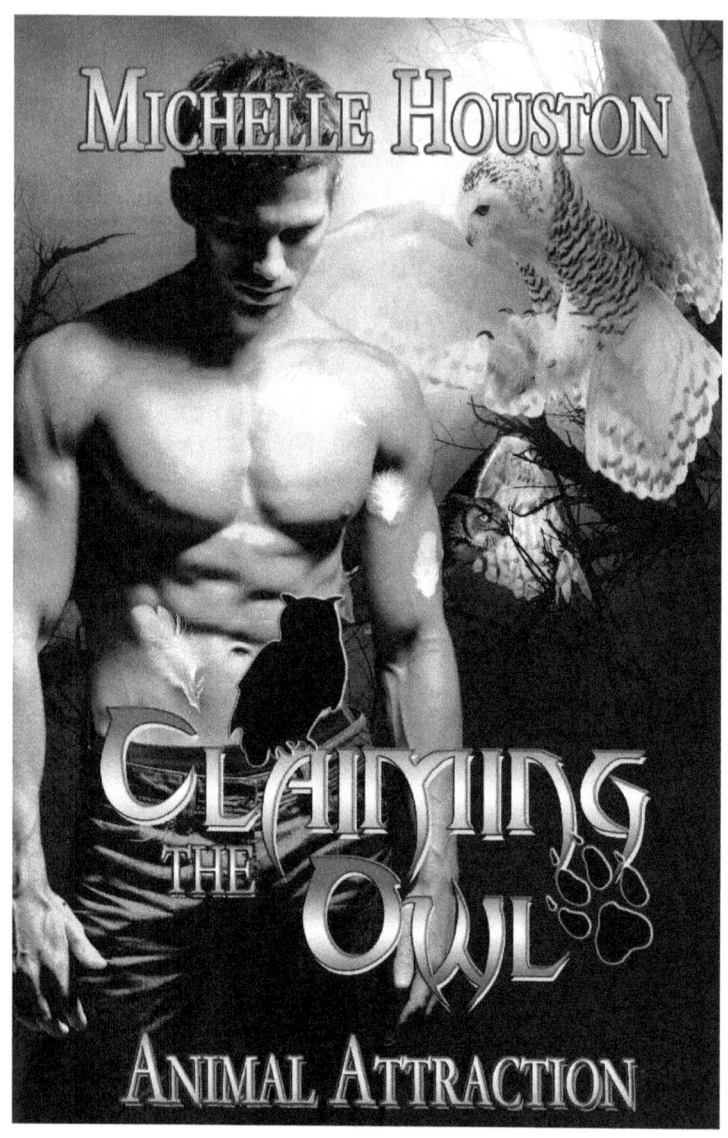

CLAIMING THE OWL

Adam watched the blond haired man casually look around his surroundings. If he hadn't been so attuned to his quarry, he might have missed the minute tightening of his shoulder muscles, the sudden stiffening of his spine as he caught a strange scent on the night breeze. Ruffling his feathers, he tried to blend in to his natural surroundings and not draw any further attention to himself.

As the young shifter sped away, Adam knew he had failed. His prey had caught his scent, and was making a run for it. Winging silently through the air, he swooped over an office building and came down in an alley just ahead of where his target headed. Cursing himself in his mind as he forced a quick transformation, he reached out and grabbed the younger man as he ran past.

As they scuffled for dominance, Adam tried to keep their struggle silent to avoid alerting the humans nearby. Although his query had a good fifty pounds on him, Adam was a mean son of a bitch when he was riled, and seldom fought fair.

Two weeks of winging after the blond had gotten him to the point he was ready to strangle him if he gave him much more grief. It didn't matter that he was completely disgusted with what he had been sent to do.

Spinning him around, Adam pinned the blond against the brick wall, his arm up and against the man's neck. "It's time to stop running. Your matriarch has demanded your presence."

His quarry closed his eyes and gave a defeated sigh, all fight draining out of him as if it had never existed. Adam had a good idea why, and he forced his own feelings on the matter aside. It wasn't his place to intervene. As long as the blond was out of reach of his matriarch, his life was his to lead, but once a summons came in, everything changed. It was the way of their beasts, loyalty to kin above all.

Gritting his teeth at the guilt for succeeding in his assignment, Adam forced his thoughts away from what was right, and focused on his instinct to obey. The matriarch of a parliament's word was law, like it or not. He had been sent to bring Nick, her youngest son, in for his upcoming nuptials, and that was just what he was doing.

"Can't you just pretend you never found me?" Hope lifted the young man's voice as he opened his eyes, looking directly into Adam's. The hunter felt as if had become the hunted. Piercing blue eyes, trimmed in thick lashes, surrounded by creamy skin; Nick was attractive as sin.

As much as Adam wanted to drag the other man back to his campsite and have his way with him, he didn't dare. Betraying a matriarch came with a high price, should she choose to take offence at any delay, or worse, at his refusal to turn the other man over. Adam had a strong feeling that one night with the man standing before him wouldn't be worth the cost. It could ultimately result in his being cast out of his parliament, basically the same as death to his kind; he would be walking away from everything he had ever known. Very few risked such censure, unless it was for a mate. Some wouldn't even risk it then. Owl shifters might be predators, but unlike their animal kin, they instinctively sought out groups to live in for support. Having others to watch their backs if things went wrong helped to keep the existence of shifters a secret from the rest of the human population.

Loosening his grip, he watched for subtle signs that the other man was going to bolt.

"I'm hoping that knowing that you've been summoned, you will come along willingly, but if it comes down to it, I have cuffs and tranquilizers. I don't want to have to knock your ass out for the drive back, but I will if I have to."

Nick leaned his head back against the red brick, the light in his eyes dimming as hope left him. His fate was unavoidable, and he knew it, judging by the slump to his shoulders. "I'll come along."

Hesitantly, Adam removed his arm, expecting to have to make a quick grab for Nick, but when the other man simply stood there patiently, he allowed himself to step back.

Running his hands down his clothing, Adam smoothed out the wrinkles the change of states had caused. One of his brothers had tried once to explain to him how his body transformed into an owl, and why his clothing would go with him, but he got lost in the geek speak of elements, basic atomic structure, and something called the law of thermodynamics. He simply didn't care beyond knowing that he wouldn't turn into a man with feathers, or an owl wearing clothing.

It was kind of like his toaster, as long as the damn thing worked, he did not care how. Some things just didn't need to be explained, the fact that they worked was proof enough. And if it broke? Well, that's why repairmen had been invented.

Motioning for the blond to precede him, Adam followed close on his heels as they headed out of the alley and toward his car, a new model sedan he had chosen because it blended in and yet got kick-ass gas mileage.

As they settled into the car, Nick held himself stiffly, almost brittle. Adam ignored the twinge of guilt that nagged at him. He was taking the man back to what was almost a fate worse than death--a marriage of convenience with a woman he neither knew anything about, nor could he ever truly love. Just one whiff of the other man's scent had been enough to convince Adam of that; he wasn't sure how the man's own mother could ignore it.

"Look man, maybe you can talk to her and get her to change her mind." Even as he offered the token hope, Adam knew he was deluding himself. Matriarchs did not simply change their minds.

Rather than dignify the comment with a response, Nick simply snorted and turned to look out the window as Adam started the car. Used to being in the company of upset and pissed off people, it wasn't the lack of vocalization that was like nails digging under Adam's skin. Rather it was the unconscious and heady attraction he was feeling towards his target.

Nick was one fine male specimen, with an intellect that was surprising given his pampered upbringing, and Adam had been able to appreciate his mind from the first night of their dance of predator and prey.

The other man had led him on a merry chase, and had used some pretty inventive ways to hide his trail. A couple of times, Adam worried he had lost him. It was only sheer tenacity and knowing what awaited failure that had kept him going. He had fought too hard to elevate his status within the hierarchy of his new parliament to risk being banished, after his own family group had shunned him when his clutch sister took over as alpha.

For two weeks, he had circled closer slowly working his way toward backing Nick into a corner, but the blond had always seemed to be one step ahead. Until tonight.

Watching him leave the club, his normally long-legged stride slowed for some unknown reason. Adam had wondered what the other man was thinking. If he knew he was being hunted, or if he had just been damn lucky so far. The slump to his shoulders had hinted at heavy thoughts weighing on his mind.

Then came Nick's risky actions; leaving the populated areas, heading off down a street alone, passing by the alley without even looking. It almost seemed like he could not only sense him, but had wanted Adam to catch him. Or maybe that was just wishful thinking. It was entirely possible that Nick had simply been preoccupied and wasn't as careful as he should have been.

Yet given how hard he had worked to stay under the radar and out of his mother's reach, neither scenario made much sense. Nick was too smart to let his guard down and become unaware of his surroundings. The man had fought too hard to stay free to just give up willingly. Something else was going on, Adam was missing something. Unable to reason it out at the moment, he shelved the troubling thoughts and focused on his most immediate goal – getting some much needed sleep.

The ride to the campsite was made in silence as Adam struggled with his instinctive need to protect and possess the man sitting beside him. There was just something about Nick that awakened a long dormant instinct, and it was growing with each breath. Each inhalation drew more of Nick's scent into his lungs, allowing it to work its way through his body until it permeated his pores.

Thankfully, they reached the entrance to the campgrounds before he completely lost his mind and pulled over, dragged the other man into his lap, and claimed the kiss his imagination had started demanding. He could feel the phantom touch of Nick's lips parting under his, as the other man surrendered to him. It took every bit of his concentration to safely pull the car into his slot and put it into park.

His tent stood silhouetted by the moonlight shining through the trees behind it. He had purposefully chosen the campsite that was as far from the bathhouse as possible, and had been lucky enough to find a remote site without close neighbors.

Staring at his tent, it took a moment for the reality of their situation to truly sink in. They were about to share a tent together – a tight, enclosed space. Alone. Adam was pretty sure he could pound nails with this erection already. Sleep wasn't going to come easy knowing the other man was just a breath away from him in that tiny-assed little tent.

When he had chosen to bring it along, he had planned for someone who was still fighting to get away. He had chosen the tent for the very fact it was small, with only one room, and one entrance.

Now, other considerations were coming to light. Like his attraction to the feisty shifter he had been sent to retrieve. A quick glance at Nick showed the blond to be in much the same state. His hands were fisted together in his lap, highlighting the bulge under the zipper of his jeans. His eyes were closed, and his nostrils flared with each inhalation.

The heady scent of aroused male filled the car as Nick turned off the engine. The faint pings of the motor cooling down only served to enhance the rasp of their breathing as each man now struggled to keep his inner beast contained.

The demand to mate, to claim was tearing at Adam's insides, until it felt like his owl's talons were ripping his stomach apart.

"Fucking hell. You knew!" It clicked in that moment why Nick had allowed himself to be caught. Only a mate-claim could trump a matriarch's wishes, although even then she could still express her displeasure in a million and one ways. Adam knew that first hand, having supported a younger sibling's mate claim against his clutch sister's wishes. She had wanted their younger sister to marry one of her lieutenants. Instead, the mate instinct awakened with a male much lower in the hierarchy.

To protect his younger sister, Adam had stood up for her, and her mate; and had been kicked out of the parliament as punishment. Now it seemed the urge to mate was going to potentially lose him another parliament, if he allowed it to happen.

Nick's eyelids flared up and he finally turned to look at Adam. The simmering desire in them was almost enough to push him past reason. The man sitting next to him was his mate.

"Yes."

Adam waited a few moments to see if Nick would expand upon his answer. When he didn't, his own impatience overwhelmed him and he demanded, "Why the fuck did you lead me on this damn chase for the last few days if you knew?"

"At first, I didn't. It was only on the fourth day that you were upwind of me and I caught a strong enough whiff of your scent. After that, I needed to know what kind of a man you were; if you were stubborn and strong, or weak and unwilling to face a challenge. I needed to know my mate was strong."

Adam knew his arousal, mingling with his own fear of loss was making him lash out, but at the moment he couldn't stop himself. "You little shit, did you even think about anyone but yourself?"

Before Nick could answer, Adam thrust opened the car door and climbed out. He needed to think, and he couldn't do that with Nick's scent wrapping around him like silken bonds, drawing them tighter and closer together. He knew he was being unfair to Nick, but he couldn't control it. It had taken him almost five years to work his way into a firm place in the parliament—five long years of facing each day with uncertainty. Of knowing that at any moment, he could be determined to not contribute enough and be asked to leave. Acceptance into a new group wasn't always permanent. He had to prove himself to the matriarch many times over.

This was to be his final test – could he track down and bring back her wayward son. Success would earn him a place among the enforcers, those tasked with upholding the laws of the parliament. He didn't even want to think about the ramifications of failure.

Adam ran a hand through his short brown hair, leaving the strands standing up in a spiky representation of his frustration. Caught up in his inner debate, he didn't hear the other car door open, which is why he jerked when a firm hand squeezed his left shoulder.

With a start, he grabbed with his right hand, spun under the blond's right arm, and bent his hand back, pinning it in against his back. It was when Nick yelped that Adam realized he wasn't being threatened. With a quick jerk of his fingers, he let the other man go.

"Fuck. Sorry about that," Adam muttered as he stepped back. The immediate instinct to sooth his mate was almost overwhelming. He had hurt the other man, even if he hadn't registered that it was him. To his owl, that demanded immediate reaction.

The man however, was still pissed as being used, by Nick and by Nick's mother. He was faced with a no-win situation, and it frustrated him to no end.

"It's okay. I shouldn't have snuck up on you like that. I was just sitting in the car thinking, this man is my mate, and I don't even know his name. I could feel your pain, and I couldn't whisper your name as I held you, because I don't know it."

Adam bit back the urge to smile at the expression on Nick's face. The other man was cute when he was befuddled. His blue eyes seemed to almost glisten in the moonlight. As soon as the thought crossed his mind, Adam shook his head and stepped back. He had been around his mate less than two hours, and he was already waxing poetic. If he wasn't careful, this mating shit would turn him into a complete wuss.

"Adam."

Nick trilled a soft sound of approval as he stepped forward. "Adam. I like that."

Another step brought him within touching distance. Adam struggled with the dual desires; one to step back and get the hell away from the temptation the other man represented, and the other to move into the other man's space, grab hold of him, and see if his lips tasted as delicious as he smelled.

As the wind shifted direction slightly, his inner beast decided for him. Reaching out, he thrust his hand in Nick's hair and pulled him close. Despite the other man having a few pounds on him, Adam was taller and very obviously more dominant. Nick surrendered into his touch without hesitation, tipping his head back and offering his throat.

Despite being bird shifters, their animals used similar signs of submission to their canine and feline kin. Baring the throat or belly signaled submission, and showing of the teeth or tightening of the body displayed dominance.

With Nick's throat offered to him, Adam's owl took over and forced him to lean down. His teeth lightly raked along the column of Nick's throat, slowly tasting the other man. It was only after he could feel his owl ruffling his feathers in satisfaction that Adam was able to take over again, and move his lips up to taste Nick's.

At the first brush of their lips, sensation burst over Adam's body. Every nerve ending fired in rapid spurts, sending a euphoric rush of chemicals throughout his system. The heady smell of Nick mixed with the earthy tang of the woods around them was intoxicating.

He had to have more. Thrusting his tongue into Nick's mouth, he teased his mate's tongue to stroke along his. It was a heady feeling, holding the blond against him, knowing their scents were intertwining until another shifter wouldn't be able to tell one from the other.

Adam jerked away as that thought entered his mind. "Shit!" Already he could smell the changes in his own scent, as well as Nick's.

Stalking off, he ran his trembling hands through his hair. Everything was changing, and he wasn't certain yet what he wanted to do about it. If anything.

"Talk to me Adam. You're my mate, what's holding you back?" Hearing the sadness in his mate's voice almost drove him to his knees.

Adam forced himself to face his mate as he revealed his own weakness. "I don't know if I can do this."

"Do what?"

"This, damnit. Mate with you. Claim you. Your mother sent me to bring you back for your marriage, not claim you for my own."

Nick moved closer, his hands slowly rising to press against Adam's chest. The touch was like a brand, heating his skin. "My mother will understand. Finding a mate is special."

"Yeah, but there's no guarantee she won't kick my ass out of the parliament. I've already lost my place once, due to a mate bond. I don't know if I can risk it again."

Nick cocked his head to the side and studied him. His pupils dilated as his owl pushed to the surface, and Adam fought his own beast's desire to rise up and rub its feathers along Nick's. At the same time, it felt like Nick was seeing into his soul; all of the empty places, the holes where his family used to be.

He had been alone for so long. The very idea of a mate of his own was something he had given up hope for ever having, and it was cruel fate to offer it now, when he was so close to belonging again.

"Tell me what happened."

Adam wanted to push the other man away, but he couldn't. Nick deserved to know just how damaged his prospective mate was. Despite being the more dominant of the two, Adam worried he was also the more scared. Certainly, Nick faced losing a lot if his mother objected to their mating. He could be cast out, and have to find a place in a new parliament.

Having been there once before, Adam wouldn't wish that on anyone. What's more, he wasn't sure he was strong enough to face the risk to himself a second time.

Moving away from his mate, he sat down on a nearby tree stump and in starts and stops, explained how he had come to be cast out by his matriarch. His own sister. During his tale, Nick came to sit on the ground at his feet and leaned against his leg, silently offering his support. Somehow, their hands had become clasped and their fingers intertwined.

"…so your mother accepted me into your parliament, and I am one task away from a permanent post as an enforcer."

"Five years you have been there, right under my mother's wing and I didn't know it." With a sigh, Nick leaned his head back against Adam's leg and closed his eyes. "If I had just come home at some time over the last few years, I would have found you and we wouldn't be where we are."

Nick rubbed his cheek along Adam's inner thigh. Looking down into his mate's face, Adam accepted the inevitable. His owl wasn't going to let this fallen angel get away, and the man wasn't strong enough to fight the animal's demands. Not when they were also his own secret desires. Nick was everything he had always wanted.

"I swear on my honor, I will return home to my parliament." As Nick spoke, his eyelids flickered open and Adam found himself staring into determined blue eyes.

Even before the other man started to speak again, Adam knew what was coming. "I will do as my mother has demanded …"

Adam pressed his index finger to Nick's lips, halting the flow of words. "You will return as your mother has demanded, and we will tell her together that we are mates, and that she will have to find someone else to marry off to form her alliance with the Dawn-Sky Parliament. I claim you for my own, Nick Night, son of the matriarch of the Snowfall Parliament."

Leaning down, Adam replaced his finger with his lips. As the more dominant of the pair, he thrilled in the softening of Nick's body against his. His mate was giving him his submission, was accepting the bond between them. With his acceptance, the last barrier to the mate-bond melted away and the silken strands that had already started to bind them together strengthened. Before, they could have broken free of each other, by their mutual acceptance, they cemented the bond.

Adam could feel Nick's joy, his arousal, and his fear of what would happen when he returned home. In turn, he knew Nick could also feel his own emotions.

Breaking the kiss, he whispered softly into the night, "Whatever happens, happens. For now, we should have no other thoughts but each other and the joy of our bond." Following his own advice was hard, but he forced the worries of the coming tumult from his head and stood. Reaching down, he clasped Nick's hand, and pulled the other man to his feet. Together, they walked towards the tent and climbed in.

It was a tight fit, but kneeling facing each other, they were able to continue to kiss as they undressed. Adam could feel Nick's hands trembling as he worked the material of his T-shirt from his jeans and pulled it up and over his head. He delighted in knowing the pleasure Nick found in his chest. It was one thing to feel attractive to a lover, but something else completely to know his mate found him desirable.

The blond slowly stroked his hands down the sleek muscles, tracing along the upper edge of each rib as he slowly worked his way down to the faint trail of hair that disappeared into the band of his jeans. His gaze lifted to meet Adam's as he worked the button free and slid the zipper down. Looking into blue eyes that were almost black with need, Adam fought against the urge to rip the clothes from his mate and join them together.

The tone that he set tonight would impact the rest of their lives together, and he wasn't about to rush things. Curling his fingers into fists, he held his arms still at his sides as Nick pushed his jeans down his hips. It was torture, holding himself still while his mate explored his body, especially when he started stroking a fingertip along the vein that throbbed in his cock. A quick glance down almost stole his control away. Nick had shifted positions and was bending over his cock, his breath whispering along the sensitive skin with each exhalation. But it was the transfixed look on his face that almost did Adam in.

Nick was looking at his cock like it was a precious treasure to be savored and enjoyed. Feeling the warm velvet stroke of Nick's tongue along the bottom of his cock startled a growl from him. It was becoming harder and harder for him to hold back, to let Nick set the pace. His owl was demanding he take over and claim their mate.

The wait was worth it as Nick wrapped his lips around Adam's cock and sucked him into the moist heat of his mouth. Eyes clamped shut at the sudden surge of pleasure, Adam struggled to hold back the rush of his orgasm. Feeling his mate's joy in his taste, in the feel of his cock, was almost enough to send him reeling.

"Enough," he bit out. Nick curled his tongue around Adam's cock and slowly moved back, teasing to the last moment. As he sat back up, Nick's gaze met his and Adam finally lost control of his animal instincts. Trilling softly, he pushed the other man onto his back and loomed over him. "I'd remove those clothes really quick if you want to have anything to wear tomorrow."

Excitement weaved through the desire on Nick's end of the bond. Adam could feel his mate's secret joy at having pushed him to the edge. He thrilled in knowing his mate wanted him with a violent intensity. Which made holding onto his shattered control even harder, but somehow Adam managed to get his own jeans and shoes off.

As Nick wiggled and squirmed in the small space to remove his jeans, Adam watched as with each movement, the blond's cock bobbed and jerked in the nest of soft curls that surrounded it. Nick's pubic hair was so light it almost looked like silver threads in the darkness.

Unable to resist, Adam leaned down and licked the smooth skin of his mate's erection. Curling his tongue around the tip, he savored his first taste of Nick's pre-come. He tasted of the night and the woods, with a hint of winter. A dark musk that sensitized each taste bud it came into contact with. For a brief moment, Adam was reminded of snowball fights with family, of his first solo flight through the woods.

It reminded him that whatever came of their mating, Nick was home to him.

When they were both naked, there was a sense of the surreal as they just looked at each other. Adam couldn't believe that after so long being alone, he was gazing upon his mate, who was unknown to him not so long before. A surge of fear for the future almost overwhelmed him, but he forced it back, unwilling to mar what should be a beautiful moment they would both remember for the rest of their lives.

Moonlight glistened through the tent netting of the roof, highlighting the delicate paleness of Nick's skin. Lying there, he was perfection in physical form. That thought was followed immediately by the wry realization that indeed he was going to be turned into a pussy by his mate, because the only words he could think of to describe the perfection he saw was in poetic terms.

Nick's knowing gaze met his and then his mate did something that shook him to his very animalistic core. With a soft smile, Nick rolled over, presenting his back to his mate. Kneeling there in the darkness, he offered his submission.

Adam's heart clenched at the emotions flooding him. He reached out and stroked his hands over the smooth skin of his lover's back and butt, feeling the muscles twitch under his touch. Nick trembled, soft trills of pleasure sounding in the silence of the night.

"Claim me." The soft spoken words were almost drowned out by the beating of Adam's heart, but he felt the ripple through their bond. His mate wanted to join with him, to complete their bond in the most elemental way. Unable to resist the lure, Adam curled his body over his mate, letting their scents mingle and seep into each other's skin.

Shifting slightly, he rocked against Nick, sliding his cock slowly back and forth over his lover's balls and up to his anus, leaving a trail of pre-come. With each motion, Nick rocked back into him.

Reaching around Nick's hip, Adam slid his hand down until he could grasp his lover's erection. With a firm grip, he started to work his hand up and down, each motion intended to learn his mate's pleasure. He could sense through their bond when his grip was just tight enough, catching that faint hint of pleasurable pain that caused Nick's breath to rush out of him on a moan.

Aware his own cock was throbbing for completion, Adam continued the sensual torture as long as he could, before having to pull back. Reaching to the corner of the tent, he grabbed the first aid kit and pulled out the only lubricant he had on hand, a small jar of petroleum jelly. While smearing it liberally on his cock, he had to pause occasionally to grip himself tight, fighting the surge of his orgasm. With each breath he took, he inhaled the heady scent of male arousal and the blended mating scent of their bodies. Each pulsation of his heart was in perfect time to his mate's.

Dipping two fingers into the jelly, he moved behind Nick again and slowly worked them into his anus. The muscles clenched and relaxed in time to the thrusts of his fingers. Nick leaned forward and laid his head against Adam's pillow and relaxed his body. Soft trills filled the tent as Nick's owl pushed closer to the surface, wanting to feel the touch of its mate. Adam could feel his own owl surging upward, demanding he claim what was theirs.

It was the softly spoken, "please," that finally broke his resolve to go slow. He shifted forward and carefully replaced his fingers with his cock. Gripping Nick's hips in his hands, he thrust forward, sliding into the velvet depths of his lover's ass. As he pulled back, the muscles surrounded his erection clenched tight, sending a wave of euphoria along his nerve endings.

Thrusting back into Nick's anus, he thrilled in the emotions flowing through their bond, the pleasure his mate was feeling as they were joined together. Adam knew the moment Nick reached down and started to stroke his own cock; he could feel the phantom sensations along his skin. Settling into a rhythm older than time, he worked his cock in and out of his lover's ass, each thrust driving them both closer to orgasm. As much as he wanted to prolong things, and spend hours learning his mate's body, the demands of the mating wouldn't let him.

He had heard that the first few times after the bond formed were quick, as each partner adjusted to feeling the other's pleasure, which magnified their own. It made every sexual event in his life pale by comparison. Being inside

Nick was a miracle of sensation, the pleasure almost too intense to be survivable.

Adam could feel his balls tightening, his orgasm building, until he couldn't control his own body he was so wrapped up in need. His animal instincts kicked in and his thrusts grew shorter and faster as he worked them both closer to the brink of climax.

Soft moans and gasps sounded in the night as both men grew closer together, their bond tightening to the point that when Nick lost the battle and his orgasm rushed over him, Adam's balls tightened, and his cock jerked as he came deep in his lover's ass.

The rush of orgasm was magnified tenfold, as his own sensations were shared with Nick, and came back to him joined with what his mate was feeling. Panting for breath, he collapsed against Nick's back, both of them slumping to the ground. He just barely had the energy left to lean to the side so that he curled around Nick, instead of flattening him.

"Holy … shit …" Adam managed to get out between gasps, as his pulse and breathing slowly returned to their normal pace several minutes later. Nick rolled over and curled against his chest, laying his head right over Adam's heart.

"Um, yeah." Adam couldn't help smiling at his mate's sleepy response. Looking down, he could see the faint white crescents Nick's eyelashes made against his skin as he lay there with his eyes closed, slipping into sleep. Feeling at peace for the first time in five years, Adam let his own eyes close and surrendered to sleep.

The next morning, amidst kisses and leisurely caresses, Adam managed to pack up the tent while Nick loaded everything into the car. After they piled in, he needed a few moments after he put the key into the ignition and started the car to still his hands, which were shaking.

"It's ok, Adam. Whatever my mother decides, we will face it together." Nick's fingers on his left hand entwined with his right, and together they put the car into drive. Neither let go of the other during the three-hour drive. Occasionally, one would try to start a conversation, but they could both feel the other's tension through the bond, and finally they settled for companionable silence.

As Adam made the final turn onto the long driveway that led to the matriarch's home, he could feel his body tensing. Nick sent waves of affection and love through the bond. He didn't want to let go of the blond's hand, but Adam had to in order to put the car into park and turn off the ignition.

Looking over at the man who had come to mean so much to him in such a short time, he leaned down and they shared a soft kiss. "Together," he whispered against Nick's lips, and received the same vow back.

His movements controlled, Adam climbed out of the car and moved around to his mate's side, to open the door for him. It was instinctive, the more dominant partner needing to survey the landscape before letting its mate out into the open. A soft trickle of sensation cascaded over him as he reached inside, offering his hand to his mate.

Clasping their hands together, they moved to the house, where the matriarch was waiting on the porch. Long silver white hair cascaded down her back, her face a feminine version of Nick's features. Neither man could read her emotion as she stared them down.

Several members of the parliament exited the house to join their matriarch. Judging by those present, a full council meeting had been in session.

"I believe I sent you to bring back my son for his upcoming nuptials, not claim him for yourself."

Shifting so that he stood slightly in front of his mate, Adam was prepared to protect him, even at the cost of his own life. His owl ruffled his feathers deep inside, offering silent support. Their mating was what mattered.

A soft trill sounded behind him, moments before Nick rubbed his face along Adam's shoulder blade.

"Yes, Matriarch. If I may speak freely?"

At a regal nod that would have done a queen proud, Adam closed his eyes for a moment and centered his thoughts. Two heartbeats passed, and he opened his eyes and met the gaze of his alpha.

Many would take it as a challenge for dominance. Around him, he could hear members of the parliament murmuring and shifting restlessly as they waited to see how the matriarch reacted.

"I had every intention of doing as you decreed, even if personally I detest the idea of arranged marriages. However, Nick turned out not to just be your son, but also my mate. And as such, I am willing to face the consequences of your anger, but I am not about to turn my back on him."

A wave of affection rushed over him as Nick trilled softly behind him. He could hear their heartbeats starting to fall into the same rhythm. Firm fingers clasped his hand, and Nick moved to stand next to him, his chin up as he met his mother's gaze.

Adam gently squeezed his mate's hand in support, knowing how hard it had to be for the more submissive man to not lower his gaze. It didn't matter that he was facing his mother, in that moment, she was his alpha.

Struggling with each breath not to submit, Adam forced the needed words out of his tight throat. "Regardless of what parliament we reside among, he is my future."

The light blue gaze of his alpha held his as silence fell. He fought the urge to look away, to submit to her dominance. In everything else, he would bow down, but not when it came to his mate.

He could feel faint tremors coursing through Nick's body, and he had never been prouder of someone in his life. It was taking everything his mate had to continue to meet his mother's gaze, to not give in to the subtle demands. "And Adam is my future as well Matriarch. He is a strong addition to our parliament, and a worth addition to our family."

Adam startled at Nick's words. Regardless of the maternal bond, he was addressing his alpha.

Silence fell as they waited to see what their matriarch would do. Adam had, after all, disobeyed her. And family bond or not, he had already experienced first hand the anger of an alpha who felt disrespected. Yet still he held her gaze, the mating bond treading between him and Nick growing stronger with each heart beat as they lent each other their support. Whatever she decided, it didn't matter. They would be together, and face whatever the future held, as one.

"My youngest son is a handful. A beautiful, precious handful. You certainly have your work cut out for you … Enforcer."

Several of the parliament members around them drew in startled breaths while other clapped or cheered. It took a moment for Adam to register why. Surely they wouldn't be happy at members being removed.

He wanted to ask her to repeat what she had said. It took Nick turning towards him and rubbing his cheek along his throat before it started to click in his dazed mind.

As realization of what she had said set in, Adam dropped his gaze, surrendering once again to her dominance. He remained still, offering her the respect and submission her position demanded. But that wasn't the only reason why. He could feel the love and affection Nick had for his mother flowing through their bond.

"Dismissed Enforcer. Enjoy some time alone with your mate. We will begin planning the official joining in three days time, after you had a chance to adjust to the idea."

Feeling the surge of need along the bond between him and his mate, he turned and met Nick's lips. Desire, affection, and love flowed between then as the final strands of their bond solidified, ties that only death could break. Finally, Adam was home.

If you enjoyed these stories, you might also like:

BLACKOUT

It's hell being in love with someone who doesn't know you're alive. Or rather, who doesn't see you as anything more than an employee. Just when he worked up the nerve to give his notice, a blackout trapped Alec with his boss, leaving him to explain to Nicholas why he has to leave a job he loves -- because he loves his boss more. He had it all worked out, except for Nicholas' reaction.

BLOOD SLAVE

Sometime in the near future, vampires have been found to exist and have been hunted down and systematically infected with a virus that causes them to lose their sight. But they have found a way around it, through the use of blood slaves.

WHERE THE BLIND LEADS: Brandon is one of those possible slaves, and if his interview goes right, he will become his master's new eyes, food supply, and lover. After his master is done whipping him and testing his sexual abilities.

LEADING THE BLIND: Nicholas used to be one of those slaves, but through the slow infection of the virus, he has been turned. Now he is facing a future he knows nothing about-- dominating another. His old master decides to step in a find a new master for Nicholas, a mortal man who is not only willing to dominate a blind vampire, but also to be his blood slave.

* * *

ABOUT THE AUTHOR

Born to ride on the back of dragons, to journey among the stars in a ship traveling faster than light, or to dance the night away in the arms of a mysterious vampire, Michelle Houston willingly shares the worlds in her mind in an effort to bring them to life.

Writing everything from short and sweet stories, to hot and spicy tales of kink, from contemporary tales of erotic romance to erotica romances featuring Greek gods, vampires and were-creatures, she has crossed sexualities and has gone wherever her mental muse has guided her, a journey she has never regretted.

As for the more mundane details: Michelle is a Sagittarius, born in the Chinese zodiac Year of the Horse. She currently resides in the Midwest US with her husband and daughter. Michelle has a love of the natural world around us (except for insects, spiders, snakes, scorpions, and she reserves the right to add more at any time). She's one of those people that actually liked Biology in High School, and enjoys learning about all things science.

In other words, she is an ordinary woman with an imagination that is only held in bounds by how fast she can type.

You can find out more about Michelle Houston on her author website at: www.michellehouston.com